DIE LIKE A MAN

Buck Langtry was a small-time rancher on Spanish Grant land and the big ranchers of the Melody Creek Valley Cattlemen's Association simply didn't trust him — his spread was too close to outlaw country, and he had a liking for Mexicans. Langtry just went his own way, and it was one of his biggest mistakes. One he paid for in blood and gunsmoke. But when he squared the debt, everyone just wished to hell they'd left him alone in the first place.

Books by Clayton Nash
in the Linford Western Library:

DAKOTA WOLF
LONG-RIDING MAN
THE MUSTANG STRIP
BRAZOS STATION

CLAYTON NASH

DIE LIKE A MAN

Complete and Unabridged

LINFORD
Leicester

First published in Great Britain in 1998 by
Robert Hale Limited
London

First Linford Edition
published 2000
by arrangement with
Robert Hale Limited
London

British Library CIP Data

Nash, Clayton
  Die like a man.—Large print ed.—
Linford western library
  1. Western stories
  2. Large type books
  I. Title
  823.9'14 [F]

ISBN 0–7089–5684–X

Published by
F. A. Thorpe (Publishing) Ltd.
Anstey, Leicestershire

Set by Words & Graphics Ltd.
Anstey, Leicestershire
Printed and bound in Great Britain by
T. J. International Ltd., Padstow, Cornwall

This book is printed on acid-free paper

1

Langtry

Buck Langtry had always been a loner — a 'holdout', as Lief Andersen called him — and that was what caused the trouble in Melody Creek valley.

Mitch Tyrell had formed the M.C.V. Cattlemen's Association, bringing in as many ranches as he could, but only those of a certain size. The association had no use for the smalltimers and, while this strictly included Langtry's Ripple L spread, while he didn't have all that many cows, he did have a large area of land. Something to do with a Spanish grant way back in his ancestry that unlocked hundreds of acres not able to be touched by the other men of the valley.

This caused some resentment and ostracism, though Tyrell left his options open by always being civil to Langtry and, once or twice, sending over men to help out when needed.

The fact that Langtry refused the help — politely enough but mighty firm — caused something of an upset amongst the association members, but still Tyrell held back his anger. He figured one day he might be able to talk Langtry into selling him some of that unused range — at a price nominated by Tyrell himself. As his large Flying T bordered the Ripple L it seemed to make sense.

But then came what was to be known as the Big Drive, from the valley clear across half-a-dozen counties, and through dangerous country riddled with outlaws, to the first cattle-boats at Corpus Christi.

Tyrell, ever looking forward, had first suggested it and then arranged it after almost a year of negotiation with the newly formed Gulf Cattle Boat Company, of which he was one of the directors, naturally.

Now for the first time, the association offered membership to the smaller ranchers of the valley — join the M.C.V. Association and drive with the valley herds in safety to the Gulf coast, then ship to lucrative markets in New Orleans, even up the Mississippi to Baton Rouge and points north.

It would be a one-time membership only, until it was successfully — or otherwise — tested, and joining fees would be kept to a minimum. Those who couldn't come up with the ready cash would have the option of paying *after* the sale of their herds, with a small 'accounting' charge added.

Several small ranchers grabbed at the chance, but some stubbornly refused Tyrell's offer. Lief Andersen's big, square, Nordic face scowled.

'You savvy this offer won't be made to you again?' He was a towering man, six feet six inches, raw-boned, rugged as a Rio cottonwood and as unforgiving as an Apache.

The ranchers shrugged: some simply

couldn't afford to have the association's fees deducted from their sales, some didn't want anything to do with men they saw as ambitious and who would one day absorb their land — but only after *they* had done all the preliminary work.

Buck Langtry shook his head even before Mitch Tyrell had finished putting the proposition to him in his ranch yard.

Langtry was a gangling sort of man, appeared to move slowly, but there was a fluidity of muscle there that was misleading and a few men in the valley could attest to just how quickly he could move when it became necessary. He was just over six feet, taller when he wore his high-crowned hat, of course, and tipped the scales at around 175. His wrists were thick and his hands large and work-hardened. He wore his sixgun carelessly — but he always wore it. A fact of which not everyone took notice. Now, his fair stubble catching the sun and seeming to glow around his square jaw, Langtry held his clear blue eyes to Mitch Tyrell's face and waited for the man's words to trail off.

'I'll drive my own herds, Mitch. Obliged for the offer but I prefer to go my own way.'

Tyrell, a man in his late forties, at least ten years Langtry's senior, tightened his thickish lips. 'Buck, I'm trying to do you a favour.'

Langtry held up one hand. 'Don't care to be beholden to any man, Mitch . . . I've got it all planned. I'll bring my herd to Corpus Christi myself.'

'The hell makes you think you'll be able to ship on the boats, Langtry?' growled Lief Andersen, early forties, aggressive, bone-headed at times. Like now. He saw Tyrell frown warningly, but he stubbornly refused to back off. 'You're too good to join the association, why the hell should we make our cattle-boats available to you?'

Langtry swung his blue eyes lazily to Andersen. He was known as 'Swede' in the valley, but only by men he favoured.

All others he preferred, and in some cases insisted, they call him 'Mister' Andersen.

'Wouldn't be good business for your boats to refuse shipment of cows, Swede. Not if they've got room.'

Andersen flushed. 'Mebbe we make sure we don't have room, eh?' He reverted to heavily accented American when he was angry and Tyrell moved a mite uneasily in the saddle when he recognised the signs. Langtry didn't appear perturbed.

'Still sounds like poor business sense.' He looked at Tyrell. 'That how it's gonna be, Mitch? I drive with you or I don't get to use the cattle-boats across the Gulf?'

Tyrell hedged. 'Why would you take the chance, Buck? Join us, you can ship for sure, get a bigger price.'

Langtry had a narrow face, his chiselled nose giving him an Indian or hawk-like look. Now he smiled faintly. 'With my fee for joining your association, shipping on the boats and so on, it'd soon cut into the profits. It's OK when you've got a lot of cows like you and your friends, but not economical for small-timers like me.'

'You'll always be a small-timer you think like that,' Tyrell snapped.

Anderson curled a lip under his drooping, tobacco-stained moustache. 'He *is* small-time. Except when it come to being a fool — then he's the biggest around.'

'Swede!' growled Tyrell warningly, but Langtry merely widened his smile and shook his head.

'Not so foolish as to want to mix it with you, Swede, and get my face changed by a butt from that bone-head of yours.'

'By Jesus, I show you who have the hard head, all right!'

For a big man he moved mighty fast, launched himself out of the saddle straight at Langtry. The rancher wasn't ready for that and he tried to push away from the corral fence he had been leaning against, but wasn't quite fast enough.

The Swede rammed into him, carrying him back against the fence rails. The lodgepole creaked with the impact and the breath was hammered from Langtry's lean body. His knees buckled some and Andersen clubbed two sledging blows down at his face. One skidded off the left side of Langtry's jaw, the other hit him at the base of the throat. He gagged and dropped as Andersen swung again. The big man howled as his fist smashed into a corral post and then Langtry came up from the side, snatching the now cold branding-iron he had been using on some penned cows. The Swede roared in rage and pain and charged in.

Buck Langtry slammed the branding iron across the man's big thigh. Andersen grunted, staggered a little, righted himself and came in, both massive hands reaching for Langtry. The rancher dodged, stepped around and slightly behind Andersen, smashed the branding-iron down behind Swede's knee. Andersen yelled as his leg gave way. He put down one hand to steady himself and Langtry cut his other leg from under him. Swaying on his knees, sweating face contorted in pain, the Swede tried to push upright. Langtry swung again, bending the iron across the man's head, knocking his hat halfway across the ranch yard. Swede shook his head, blinking, though his eyes were losing their lustre and there was a trickle of blood at his nostrils. Langtry unhurriedly kicked his arms from under him and the Swede rolled to the dust on his back, eyes showing white now.

He made one more attempt to get on his feet, but fell back unconscious.

The riders who had accompanied Tyrell and Andersen stirred uneasily and one man started to draw his sixgun.

The whole bunch of them froze as suddenly they were looking into the rock-steady muzzle of Buck Langtry's Peacemaker.

Later, no man there could swear he had even seen the rancher draw the weapon. It had just — appeared — in his fist.

'Don't let this get outa hand, boys,' Langtry said mildly, still hefting the bent branding-iron in his left hand. He set his gaze on Tyrell. 'Thanks for the offer, Mitch, but no thanks.'

Tyrell nodded jerkily, his face tight and grey. 'That was dirty fighting, Buck!'

Langtry shrugged, jerked his head towards the penned cattle. 'Got a lot of work to do — I didn't aim to bust my hands on the Swede's thick head. Be obliged if you'd be moving along, Mitch. *Still* got a lot of work to do.'

While some men loaded the unconscious Swede on to his horse, Tyrell squinted at Langtry. 'Where you gonna get men to help you drive your herds to the Gulf?'

'I know where I can get some.'

Tyrell waited but Langtry didn't elaborate.

'You join us, you won't have the extra cost of having to hire trail hands.'

Langtry merely smiled, shook his head. As the riders turned their mounts to leave, Tyrell said, 'By the way, Buck, you don't come with us, you don't use our trail at all. We'll see to that. Sorry, but you've brought it on yourself.'

'I know a trail.'

Tyrell scoffed. 'Only way left is through outlaw country. You'll lose every cow you take with you!'

Langtry smiled again. 'See you on the Gulf, Mitch.'

Tyrell's face showed the anger boiling within him: he was mad because he just couldn't seem to shake this goddamned small-time rancher!

Damn it, he had tamed this valley since the end of the war, he'd fought off Indians and Mexican *bandidos* and white-trash outlaws. He'd *earned* the respect of folk in this valley — and the only one who consistently showed him no respect at all was this lanky, cold-eyed Buck Langtry.

He frowned more deeply as he rode after the others, wondering why the hell it should be so important to him to have this man's respect.

He rammed home his guthook spurs, raking mercilessly at the flanks of his part-Arab black, taking perverse delight in hearing its scream of protest as he made the blood flow.

2

Wetbacks

Whoever the man was, he was in trouble.

Sheriff Cal Magill lowered the field-glasses and frowned. That *hombre* below in the dry wash was in pretty bad shape. He was trying to lug his saddle on his back, use it for shade in this wide-open parched plain that was half-brother to a desert. But there were dark stains on his clothing, a large patch just above his waistband on his ragged shirt, another between knee and hip on the left leg. He was staggering, limping, and although Magill couldn't see his face clearly because of the saddle and a dusty beard, he had the impression that it was contorted in pain.

The lawman knew the man in the

wash had had more than a fall from his horse: those dark stains looked like blood from bullet wounds to him. Which, of course, grabbed the sheriff's interest in a hammerlock and, as he replaced the fieldglasses in his saddlebags, he unsheathed his Winchester and quietly jacked a shell into the breech.

He sat amongst the boulders where he had come to check out the wash before proceeding on his way back to Laredo. This was the edge of outlaw country and he had no notion to ride slapbang into a bunch of hellions making for the sanctuary of the wild territory that even the Indians avoided.

But a lone man . . . wounded, half-dead with thirst and pain . . . well, Magill was a man who took his job seriously and if this was some wanted *hombre*, he didn't aim to pass up the chance of nailing him.

He waited, knowing that if the man had enough stamina he would stumble out of the dry wash only ten yards away and then Magill would have him dead to rights.

The only thing that made him a mite leery was that the man was packing twin sixguns. Not all that usual even along the border, but a few desperate characters did it. And mostly, he had learned the hard way over the years, they were men who knew how to shoot a Colt in either hand. The flashy ones who did it for show, well, they weren't around for long. But this man below looked to be in his thirties . . .

It took more than half an hour for the man to appear. Magill was figuring he might have collapsed somewhere in the wash and was considering going down to see, but then he appeared, still lugging the saddle, all heeled-over to one side by its weight, taking staggering little steps in efforts to stay on his feet. One of those staggering runs brought him within five yards of Magill and the lawman rose up, rifle to shoulder, and said loudly, 'Just drop the rig and grab a piece of that blue Texas sky, feller.'

The man stopped as if he had run into a brick wall, straightened painfully, the saddle sliding from his grip and down his back, slapping against his legs, setting him stumbling. He went down to one knee and only his left side was facing Magill. The man's right hand appeared holding a sixgun and the sheriff was startled by the smoothness of the draw by a man in such dire straits. But he had fired the rifle and levered in a fresh shell before his bullet tore the pistol from the man's grip.

The impact slammed the man over on to his side and he moaned as he held his tingling wrist against his chest. He coughed and his greasy, ragged-brim hat fell off, sweat-stringy hair tumbling darkly across his forehead.

The sheriff came forward slowly, sliding one foot ahead of the other, rifle angled down, covering the wounded man. He was panting now and he turned his dust-clogged, bearded face upwards, lips scaled and cracked with thirst.

'Water,' he rasped and Magill stopped a yard away, frowning deeply.

Then he leaned forward as the man croaked again and a slow smile spread over the lawman's hard-planed face.

'I don't believe it!' he said, his native Kentucky accent showing as it always did when he got excited or angry. But it wasn't anger that brought out the backwoods accent this time . . . 'Ed Largo!'

★ ★ ★

The fiesta at Nuevo Laredo had taken its toll on Buck Langtry and the men who now rode with him back towards the border.

Tequila and *pulque* and the powerful Mexican tobacco had left him with a taste and rawness in his mouth and throat that made him feel as if he had just walked through a brushfire. The Mexicans riding silently behind didn't look as bad as he felt, but they had had a lot more practice at suffering in silence than he had.

Most of the six riders claimed some sort of kinship to Langtry, by complicated marriage lines that went way back to the time of the *conquistadores*. Somewhere back there, one of his migrating British ancestors had married a Spanish *señorita*, daughter of a *ranchero* whose life he had saved from a maddened bull. As years went by the *hidalgo*'s four sons died by violence in one way or another, so that when it was time for the *ranchero* himself to slip his mortal coil, he had only the English son-in-law to will his vast Texas holdings to. They passed down through the family for hundreds of years until Langtry finished up with what remained of the original holdings and which was now his Ripple L ranch.

But cousins and second-cousins and third- and fourth-cousins lived below the Rio Grande and from time to time he visited them or they him.

In the past, he had helped them out in their troubles, financially when he was able, with muscle — or gunsmoke — when it was necessary.

Buck Langtry was a mighty popular *hombre* with the Mexican branch of his family and when he needed some men to help him drive his herds through dangerous country to Corpus Christi he knew where to go.

He had been prepared for the inevitable fiesta but the hang-over was even worse than he had anticipated.

'Must be getting old,' he decided, speaking half aloud, causing young Raoul riding alongside to query him. But he only shook his head — gently — and lifted a hand, indicating that he would rather not talk.

Raoul grinned; a slim, hawk-faced man in his early twenties. He leaned from the saddle and clapped Langtry on the back, causing the man to sway wildly, startled, coughing and hawking. The Mexican's grin widened. '*Si*, you are right, *primo*. The old age she catch up with you, eh?' He laughed, hipped in saddle and spoke rapid Spanish to his companions.

Langtry winced and clapped his hands over his ears as they roared with laughter. 'You sadistic bastards!' he growled, but gave a sour grin a few moments later as they came to a stream and splashed across.

He dismounted slowly and flopped into the shallows, letting the cool waters flow over him, turning his face this way and that, rinsing out his mouth, swallowing a little.

The others also wet bandannas and wiped their faces or poured water over their heads. They found a stand of trees where they sat in the shade and Langtry rolled a cigarette with shaking hands, refusing the hand-rolled, home-grown cheroots favoured by the others.

'We bring plenty of tequila with us, *primo*,' a middle-aged Mexican named Diego said with a grin. 'You like a bite of the dog, eh . . . ?'

Langtry looked away, waving a negative hand. 'What I'd like is to sleep for a couple of days and mebbe I'll do that when we get back to the ranch — while you *sadistas* round-up my herds and get them ready for the trail.'

Grey-stubbled, fat little Pancho slapped Langtry across the shoulders, making him spill his tobacco. '*Bueno*! Then we 'ave fiesta to make sure we 'ave good trail drive, eh?'

The others reckoned that was a good idea and Langtry groaned, wondering how come his brain had slipped a cog so badly that he'd ever come up with the idea of bringing in these men to help him out.

When they rode into Ripple L, the Mexicans spurring ahead, letting out exuberant yells, raising a choking dust cloud, Langtry hauled rein as he saw the man waiting on his porch. Lester, his bronc-buster came hurrying out of the barn, holding a bridle he had been repairing.

'It's Sheriff Magill, boss,' Lester said, a slim, horse-faced man that some men swore could talk to horses in their own lingo. 'Been waitin' almost a day for

21

you. Won't say why.'

The Mexicans ignored the lawman, still riding and showing-off amongst themselves, but Langtry climbed down carefully from his saddle and walked stiffly up to the porch.

Cal Magill was smoking his pipe and made no effort to rise as he studied the rancher's ravaged face.

'That gen-ew-ine greaser tequila been at you again? Or was it t'other way round, Buck?'

Langtry worked up a miserable attempt at a smile. 'Either way, I'm the loser. What can I do for you, Cal?'

'Well, I could use a cup of java and some hot biscuits. Belly's sittin' on my spine but your ranch hands don't seem to want to take time off for lunch.'

'Busy time, round-up, and getting the herd ready.'

The lawman slid his gaze to the Mexicans who were slowing down their antics now, some dismounting. 'Yeah — Kinfolk?'

'Yeah.'

'Still wetbacks, Buck. They got no right to be here, workin' at a job Americans can do.'

Langtry tensed, forcing his addled brain to concentrate. 'Is this why you're waiting for me?'

'Mebbe part of it. More a personal view, I guess. I don't go along with this kinda thing, Buck.'

Langtry held the man's hard gaze. 'They're kin on a visit. If they want to help me out around the spread, I don't see that it's any business of yours, Cal.'

Magill nodded soberly. 'We-ell, we'll push that pot to the back of the stove for now. What I come out for is to take you back to jail.'

Langtry stiffened. 'What?'

Magill sighed, tamped down his coal of tobacco in his pipe bowl. 'You assaulted Swede Andersen, cracked two of his ribs, busted-up his leg so's he's gotta use a stick to get around. He wants you charged, Buck.'

'The Swede? He's calling in the law just because . . .?' Langtry's raspy voice trailed off. His mouth tightened. 'No, it's not that little go-round we had at all, is it? It's to keep me from getting my herd ready for the trail to Corpus Christi. I figure the association's behind this, Cal.'

'Figure what you like. I know nothin' about the association, only that Swede swore out an official complaint and I'm takin' you in and holdin' you in jail till Judge Le May gets good and ready to hear the complaint in court.'

Langtry cursed. 'The sons of bitches! This is their way of getting back at me. Look, Cal, I'll be there when the judge holds court, but I'll pay the bail now so's I can get my herd ready and Raoul and Diego can start the drive while I sort things out with the judge, OK?'

Cal Magill tapped out his pipe on the arm of the porch chair and stood slowly, taking his time to look around at the rancher. 'No, it ain't all right . . . might've been if you'd come back alone, but bringin' in these greasers, well, it don't seem legit to me.'

Langtry held down his rising anger, watching his kinfolk off-saddle down by the corral. 'You gonna arrest 'em, Cal? Didn't know your jail was big enough to hold 'em.'

Magill's eyes narrowed. 'If I want it to be, it'll be big enough — no matter how many I have to cram in. But, no, they can stay put here on your spread. 'Long as they don't move off your land, they won't get no argument from me — leastways, not till Judge Le May makes a rulin'.' He smiled crookedly. 'Meantimes, I'll hold you.'

Langtry stared coldly as the lawman drew his sixgun. 'They got to you, huh?'

Magill kept his face blank. 'How's that?'

'Mitch Tyrell, the Swede — the association. They got to you. Told you to hassle me, make sure I'm delayed getting my herd on the way to Corpus Christi. Slipped you a double eagle, huh?'

'No one *got* to me!' gritted the lawman. 'I'm my own man — an' ridin'

25

mighty high right now. Guess you ain't heard.'

Langtry waited, refusing to play Magill's game, but his aching brain was trying to cope with this unexpected deal.

'Guess you never heard I brought in Ed Largo, day before yest'y, likely while you was carousin' south of the border.'

Langtry stiffened. Ed Largo was the most Wanted man in Texas — and New Mexico and Colorado and a few other states or territories. He was a killer for hire, an outlaw from way back, with wanted dodgers yellowing and rotting on law-office walls all over the southern part of the States.

'That's a feather in your hat, all right, Cal,' Langtry allowed. 'How'd you manage that?'

Magill's chest seemed to have swelled up some by now. 'Had me a piece of luck, found him plumb tuckered-out and wounded on the edge of the badlands. Din' even put up a fight: was glad to see me, I reckon — '

'Bet he's changed his mind by now.'

'You'd win if you made that bet. He was totin' a little lead but nothin' too serious. Hoss had rolled on him an' he says a coupla Injuns tried to nail him but it was likely someone from outlaw country. Don't matter. He's nailed.' Then he sobered. 'Only drawback is, me bein' law, I don't get to claim the re-ward.'

Langtry smiled thinly. 'That must hurt, Cal!'

'Damn right! It's more'n ten thousand dollars in total — and that's just the papers I got on him. Could be a couple more from California, I hear.' Scowling, Magill reached out and lifted Langtry's sixgun from his holster. 'You can ask him if you like. You're gonna get the chance; you'll be in the cell right next to him . . . '

They both looked up at the sound of gravel crunching. The Mexicans were lined up, no longer boisterous or laughing. They looked very sober and their hands were close to their weapons, guns or knives. Raoul spoke.

'There is trouble, *Primo*?'

Langtry nodded. 'Some. Sheriff don't like you being here, but I don't think there's a lot he can do about it 'long as you stay on Ripple L. Other thing is that little waltz I told you I had with the Swede before visiting you: he's charging me with assault and I got to wait for the judge in jail.'

Raoul, Diego and Pancho exchanged knowing glances. The fat little Pancho said, looking amazingly innocent for one with such a devilish face, 'Then we will round-up your *ganados* and 'ave them ready for the trail when you return, eh?'

'You just stay put!' Magill growled. 'You're here on a visit accordin' to Buck, so you just enjoy the scenery or whatever. You ain't here to work.'

Diego spread his hands. 'Work, *Señor* Sheriff?' He grimaced and shrugged expressively. 'What is work to one man is play to another, eh? We are *vaqueros*. We love to ride — and round-up cattle.

We would be bored if we did nothing but sit around . . . '

'Listen, you, don't try that greaser talk on me! I said you don't work while you're here, and by hell you blamed well *don't!*'

Diego held the lawman's gaze. 'Whatever we do *on Buck's rancho* will not be work, *señor*. It will be fun, relaxation for us. Surely your *norteamericano* law cannot stop a man having a little harmless fun on private land? Aiye, even in Mexico this does not happen.'

Magill's nostrils were pinched and his chest was heaving. He glared at the Mexicans, glared at Langtry.

'Smart-ass greasers! All right, Buck, the hell with this. *You're* gonna be locked up so it don't much matter what these goddamn wetbacks get up to, does it?'

Langtry turned to the Mexicans and spoke rapidly in Spanish, too fast for the lawman to follow. When Magill demanded to know what he had told his 'cousins' he merely shrugged.

'Said for 'em to make themselves to home, that I'd be back soon's I could.'

'You took a helluva long while to say that!'

Langtry smiled. 'Spanish is that kinda lingo, Cal, takes the long way round. Those old *dons* enjoyed using words . . .'

'You throw a saddle on a fresh bronc and let's get on into town. I've had a bellyful of this.'

'*Hasta la vista, amigos*,' Langtry called to the Mexicans.

'We will await your return, *primo*,' Raoul said quietly and Magill snorted.

'Don't hold your breath!'

3

Cellmates

So this is Ed Largo, Langtry thought as the sheriff closed the cell door behind him. He looked through the upright bars dividing the two cells at the big man sprawled on the bunk next door.

Largo was propped up on one elbow and threw Langtry a look of pure contempt. He settled down on his back uninterestedly, grimacing a little as he moved to get into a comfortable position with his wounds. Magill had had the sawbones tend to them and white bandages showed beneath the killer's shirt through a rent in the cloth no doubt made by the bullet that had wounded him.

His left thigh was heavily bandaged, too, the white cloth showing where the doctor had slit the trousers.

'How you like him?' Magill asked Langtry, still some excited that he actually had the notorious killer behind bars in his own cell block. 'Don't look so much, all dirty and down that way, does he? Stories they tell about Ed Largo you kinda got the notion he's ten feet tall and half as wide across the shoulders. You ask me, he's wide between the ears with a whole lot of nothin' in between.'

Largo, drawing on his cigarillo, blew smoke towards the high ceiling, ignored the lawman.

'You want anythin', Buck, just holler.' Magill pulled his lips back from his teeth in a tight grin. 'Don't mean I'll hear you, of course!'

'Enjoy your day, Cal,' Langtry called after him bitterly, as the lawman made his way down the passage towards the front office.

Langtry leaned against the bars, rolled and lit a cigarette. Largo glowered, his face coarse and scabbed now from healing gravel scars and thorn tears. He had thick lips and a large nose but small, frightening eyes, like looking into a screwhole in a coffin.

'The hell you lookin' at, dummy?'

Langtry drew lazily on his cigarette and shrugged. 'Sheriff said you're Ed Largo, so I guess that's what I'm looking at.'

'Then look somewheres else. I don't like people starin' at me.'

Langtry glanced around the cell. 'Mmm — ain't much of interest to look at in here. But then you ain't very interesting, either, Largo, so think I'll catch up on some shut-eye.'

'You shut your mouth, you lousy son of a bitch!' Largo was up on his elbow now. 'I'm *Ed Largo*, for Chrissakes! Don't that mean nothin' to you, dummy?'

'Sure, I've heard of you. A mean little son of a bitch with a lousy temper and only knows one way to settle anything that riles him.'

Largo swung his legs over the edge of the bunk, breath hissing through his

33

large nostrils, now. 'Listen, you, if that goddamned set of bars wasn't between us, you'd be *dead*! Hear? I'd squeeze your lousy throat till your eyes popped out on your cheeks!'

Langtry, lowering himself to his bunk, jammed his cigarette between his lips, lifted both hands and made them tremble. 'Hell, now you'll give me bad dreams, scaring me that way.'

Largo swore, loud, filthy epithets. He dragged himself across to the dividing bars, gripped them with his big hands and strained as if he would bend them. His small eyes bulged.

'You'll keep! I'll remember you, mister!'

Langtry tilted his hat forward over his face. 'Well do it quietly, OK? I'm plumb tuckered.'

Largo continued to lean against the bars, smoking jerkily, eyes blazing hate at the prone rancher whose steady breathing grew heavier and more regular until the outlaw heard the beginning of a snore coming from beneath the battered hat.

He spat into Langtry's cell. 'Yeah, you'll keep, mister! There's people won't leave me to rot in here and when I go, I'll take your pecker with me!'

Langtry snored louder and Largo smashed the heel of a fist hard enough against a bar to make it ring dully.

★ ★ ★

'You should've pushed them damn wetbacks all the way back across the border, Cal!' snapped Mitch Tyrell in the law office. 'The hell you leave them at his ranch for? They'll only round-up his cows for him.'

'They do, that's *all* they can do,' the sheriff said calmly. 'I told 'em they set foot off the Ripple L, I'll kick their butts for 'em.'

'Mitch is right,' growled Swede Andersen. 'You shoulda sent them back.'

Magill looked from one man to the other. 'Look, you wanted Langtry

35

locked up so's he'll miss shippin' his herds on the cattle-boats, right? Well, he's locked-up and Judge Le May ain't due back from San Antone for another week, so you'll be well ahead of him and the boats will've sailed before he can get there, even if the judge only fines him instead of throwin' him in jail. What's your problem, gents? I've done what you asked.'

'You were *paid*,' said the Swede. 'We expect more than this for our money.'

'You expect more, it'll cost you more,' the sheriff told them coldly. 'Now just what the hell do you expect? Langtry's out of it and I'll see the wetbacks don't move his herds. You ask me, I've given good value for money.'

Andersen started to complain, but Mitch Tyrell placed a hand on his arm. 'Cal's right, Swede. He did what we asked. All we can do is get our drive underway while Langtry rots here in jail till Le May gets back . . . and you know it could be longer than a week. Everyone knows about that prissy l'il redhead he keeps stashed away in San Antone. He won't leave her long as she's showin' him a good time.'

Swede mumbled under his breath, snapped his large head up, rubbing gently at the bruised ribs. 'I don't like these Mexes bein' on Ripple L.'

Tyrell smiled thinly. 'Well, mebbe somethin'll happen to make them leave Langtry's ranch.'

'They do and I'll come down on 'em like an avalanche!' Magill said quickly.

Tyrell's smile widened as he looked at Andersen and spread his hands. 'See?'

★   ★   ★

Langtry started out of his doze as he heard someone say his name and when he sat up on his cell bunk he was surprised to see Mitch Tyrell and Swede Andersen standing in the passage at his cell door.

'Sheriff said we could have a few words with you, Buck,' Tyrell said pleasantly enough. 'We're sorry about this but . . . '

'Quit the soft-soap,' cut in Langtry harshly, aware that Largo was watching and listening from his own cell bunk. 'What the hell're you doing to me?'

'Nothing. You brought it on yourself. There were plenty of men who saw you attack Swede with that branding-iron. He has a right to expect to see you punished by law for that.'

Langtry walked up to the door and the men took an involuntary step back across the narrow passage. In his cell, Largo showed a little more interest, narrowing his eyes as he watched Langtry more closely now.

'You're punishing me, all right, but smacking the Swede loose from his ribs was only incidental. You don't want me to make that cattle-boat, but what I can't figure is why? What the hell difference does it make to you?'

He was addressing Mitch Tyrell and the man frowned, looking mildly surprised that Langtry had taken this tack.

'Perhaps you need bringing down a peg or two, Buck,' the rancher told him curtly. 'Intentional or not, you've estranged yourself from quite a lot of folk in this valley.'

'I did that the moment I claimed my Spanish land grant.'

'Of course. But you're uppity, snooty, a loner.'

'I'll agree with the last only there, Mitch, I've always been a loner, like it that way. And I don't care for clubs or associations or whatever you like to call them. I like my independence, to make my own decisions and to live with whatever mistakes I make. That way, I'm the only one I have to answer to.'

'You haf the too much land!' blurted Swede, his homeland accent coming to the fore again and telling Langtry how upset he was on this subject. It didn't surprise him, though. He'd known all along he wasn't popular having legal title to so much land, most of which he never used, but one day, maybe, he would use it . . . or his kin would.

'Hell, is that what scares you, Mitch? That some day I'm gonna deed some or all of my land to my Mexican kin? That you might have *them* for neighbours?'

The answer was plain to see in Tyrell's flushed face. Langtry almost spat at the man's feet.

'You're a damn poor excuse for a man, Mitch! Those men on my spread right now are some of the finest cattlemen you'll ever see. They could help you, help this whole valley with what they know about raising cows in this border country. Instead of listening to them — and they would help you if they were asked, they're that kind of folk — you stir up hatred against them. Hell, the war with Mexico's long gone. Time we tried to get along.'

Tyrell took his time answering, his jaws clamping tightly, rows of knotted muscles ridging his jawline.

'I don't care about the greasers, nor their advice. But I want some of that

40

land you lay claim to, Buck. You don't get your herd to market this season and you're gonna be in serious trouble. I know, I've checked with the bank and you're already behind with payments on the loan you took out to build that dam. You sell me the land I want, and you have no more money problems.'

'I sell my herd and I'll clear that loan.'

Mitch smiled thinly. 'Sure — but that's the problem, selling your herd. First you need to get it to market and just not any old market, but one where you'll get the best price. Look, Buck, we can negotiate on this. Swede's a reasonable man. If you . . . '

He broke off, seeing the way Buck Langtry was regarding Andersen.

'So, you're a reasonable man, eh, Swede? How much is your share for being — *reasonable*?'

'You shut up!' Swede stepped forward in his anger, arm raising.

Suddenly Langtry's arm shot out, fisted up the front of the big man's shirt

41

and pulled violently. Swede wasn't fast enough to get his hands up to protect himself. He smashed face-first into the bars and, as he sagged, Langtry jerked him back, ramming his bloody face again into the bars. The man's legs buckled and he started to fall. Langtry smashed him into the iron twice more before he released his hold and allowed the semi-conscious man to sag to the floor. Mitch Tyrell, watching Langtry warily, crouched down and grabbed the Swede's ankle, pulled him back from the bars.

'You're finished now, Buck! This was a really stupid move! Now you're gonna be locked up for a long, long time! If you need money for an attorney — and you will, I can assure you! — give some thought to how much you can sell the north-west section of your land for.' Tyrell smiled crookedly. 'Then halve it, because, it's suddenly just become a buyer's market!'

He grabbed the bloody-faced Andersen under the arms and half-dragged, half-carried the man down the passage towards the front office.

Langtry watched them go, cursing himself for a fool.

In a minute, Sheriff Magill came storming in to stand in front of the cell, sixgun in hand. He was raging.

'You goddamn fool, Buck! You 'bout half-killed the Swede! He's gonna demand Judge Le May throws the book at you now . . . and I'll back him. Attackin' that way — Judas *priest!*'

'What you mean *attackin'* him?'

Both Magill and Langtry turned towards Largo who was sitting up on his bunk, ugly face hard, his gaze rock-steady.

'You sayin' this *hombre* attacked that dumb-lookin' tree with a hat on?'

'You shut your mouth, Largo, you know nothin' about this!' Magill snapped and Largo laughed sardonically.

'Oh-ho-ho. You reckon not, mister? Hell, I was just lyin' here watchin' the whole damn thing. I seen it *all.*'

43

Langtry frowned, something in Largo's tone making him suddenly mighty wary.

'An' just what did you see?' demanded the lawman.

'Hell, both them other two *hombres* jumped this feller about sellin' his land. More or less said if he didn't sell, he'd never get a chance to drive his herd to Corpus Christi and to market. Then the bank'd foreclose on some loan he took out to build a dam.'

Magill frowned. 'Yeah, everyone knows about Buck borrowin' to build that dam — which so far ain't done much for his land.'

'I wouldn't know about that. But he was standin' close to the bars, tryin' to reason with them others when the Swede hooked him a good one in the belly, right through the bars. As he doubled over, he grabbed for this feller's hair, but he missed and just as well, 'cause I could see he aimed to rap him good against the bars — '

'You're lyin'!'

Largo looked exasperated. 'Now why the hell would I lie? This *hombre's* nothin' to me one way or t'other.'

The sheriff leaned closer. 'Then why're you tellin' me all this hogwash?'

'First, it ain't hogwash and second, I don't like no so-called law-abidin', upstandin' *citizen* puttin' it to a feller like this just 'cause he's sittin' on land the citizen happens to want. Hell, it's the same kinda thing that set *me* on the owlhoot trail. Feller robbed me of my own place and because I'd done a little time for rustlin', no one believed my story an' I was gonna be jailed for seven years while that solid *citizen* moved right in on my land. So I killed him and lit-out. Lickety-split.' Largo looked at Langtry for the first time since he had started talking. 'Naturally, our friend here fought back, banged the Swede into the bars and then that other clumsy galoot, the Swede's friend, stumbled and fell on him, knockin' him into the bars again, makin' a real mess of him — ' Largo lifted a forefinger and tapped the air with it in Magill's direction. 'Now that's what happened, Sheriff, an' don't you let them two lyin' sonuvers tell you no different.' He turned to Langtry who looked sort of stunned and then grinned tightly without mirth. 'Ah, don't thank me, feller. Us convicts gotta stick together. We don't help each other, there just ain't no one to count on at all. You're welcome, friend. You want me to stand up in court and tell what really happened here, I'll gladly do it.'

Ed Largo winked and lumbered back to his bunk, holding one arm against his wounded side.

Cal Magill glared at Langtry, but there was a kind of uncertainty in his voice when he asked, 'Was he speakin' gospel?'

Buck Langtry scratched at his jaw-line, flicked his eyes towards Largo who was now stretched out on his bunk again, then back to the sheriff.

'You heard the man, Sheriff, he's got nothing to gain by lying.'

But, of course, Largo had a good deal to gain: if he could get the sheriff to believe his version of what had happened, it would mean he would be kept here in this tin-pot jail until Langtry's court case came up so he could give evidence.

And the longer he was kept away from the ironclad security of the State Penitentiary, the more chance he had of being rescued by his friends on the outside.

In fact, even if the sheriff *didn't* believe him, he would still likely have to give evidence so it could be weighed up by the jury.

Yeah. This Langtry had impressed him, too. He'd had him figured for some local bad boy who'd crossed the sheriff and the big ranchers; no great shakes at anything, a big frog in a small pool, but he liked the man's moves. Judas, the way he'd reached through those bars and grabbed that Swede! Faster than a striking rattler . . .

Yeah, he could use a man like that. Or *make* use of him.

4

Rewards

Judge Le May surprised everyone by returning from San Antonio before the end of the week. He was surly and irritable and the word was that his redhead had either kicked him out or had become impatient with the judge's tardiness in readying himself for their nightly pleasure hour.

Either way, the men who were listed to face Judge Augustus Le May in his court during the next few days began to have stomach cramps and bouts of the shakes. Even two 'regulars' up on drunk-and-disorderly were sentenced to five days each in jail and fined a hefty amount. A man who beat a saloon gal was given a surprisingly light sentence — maybe it had something to do with the girl in question being a redhead, even though her hair was dyed . . .

In any case, Mitch Tyrell and the still recuperating Swede Andersen had high hopes that the judge's sour mood would work well for them and that he would impose a severe sentence on Buck Langtry, even though that killer, Largo, was supposed to be giving evidence that would clearly make Langtry's actions no more than self-defence.

The association's herds had been on the trail to Corpus Christi for four days already so even if by some miracle Le May only fined Langtry and turned him loose, it was too late for the man to drive his own herds north. The only thing that did worry Tyrell was that he had heard rumours that Langtry's Mexican kin had the correct papers for visiting the United States. Whether these would allow them to work or not he wasn't sure, but he had his attorney working on it.

Even so, he comforted himself, the only trail left to the Mexicans, if they did drive Langtry's herds north, was now through outlaw country, for the association's combined herds would eat out all the graze available on the regular trail and his men had orders to fill in the sparse water-holes after they had used them.

Tyrell was determined he would break Langtry this time — into pieces small enough to blow away in a squirrel's sneeze . . .

The day came when the prisoners had to be moved from the jail to the crowded courthouse and it was wet and unusually cold.

A bitter wind moaned through the streets of Laredo and any folk out of doors hurried along to their destinations wrapped well in slickers or corn sacks or under umbrellas that threatened to blow inside-out at a couple of corners. The streets soon turned to mud, and yellow water frothed down the ragged gutters, the only time they were ever cleaned.

Langtry rubbed his hands briskly together in the cell and was surprised when Cal Magill appeared with five deputies. Three he recognized as townsmen or range riders who had taken a temporary law badge for the escort of himself and Ed Largo to the courthouse — and back, if necessary.

'You gonna give us slickers?' growled Largo, but Magill merely scoffed.

'Enjoy the feel of clean, cold rain, Largo, might be your last chance before you get sent up to the State Pen — or the gallows, which is what you deserve.'

Largo's small eyes slitted. 'Yeah, well, I guess we all get what we deserve sometime or other, Sher'ff.'

Langtry said nothing as the cell doors were opened and, under the cocked guns of the deputies, the prisoners stepped out into the passage. Magill hustled them close together, linked Langtry's left wrist to Largo's right one with manacles and a short length of chain. Each had their ankles shackled and their hats jammed on their heads.

'Let's not keep the good judge waitin', boys,' Magill said with a tight grin, and motioned to the deputy nearest the rear door to open it.

The man did so, resting his sawn-off shotgun against the wall while he dropped the bar and shot back the long-bolts. He heaved against the weight of the heavy, iron-bound timber and, as the door opened, gusty cold rain hammered into the passage, causing the armed men to involuntarily step back. The sheriff, prisoners and two other deputies were jostled and stumbled, cursing.

Then the door was slammed open, smashing the deputy holding it back into the adobe wall, mangling his nose and jaw. Blood-splattered face contorted with sudden pain, the man started to fall and the door was rammed into him again and the breath gusted out of him raggedly as he fell to his knees, semi-conscious.

By that time, armed men were swarming into the passage, the leader yelling, 'Watch for Largo!'

Guns blasted and filled the narrow

passage with thunder and deadly shot. A deputy nearest the door staggered, crying out in agony, going down, shuddering as two more bullets ripped into him. Magill swore and brought his big Greener around, the long barrels snagging briefly on Largo's shoulder. The killer shoved hard, staggering the sheriff, rammed the point of his shoulder into him and pushed him right into the line of fire.

Sheriff Cal Magill dropped, twisting as he fell, the Greener blasting and bringing down a shower of plaster on the remaining group.

One of the temporary deputies ran back down the passage towards the front office without firing a shot. Langtry dropped to his knees, yanked hard on the chain linking him to Largo and pulled the killer off balance. The man cursed him as he stumbled to his knees, and then they sprawled full length as the guns roared over their heads.

Two of the outlaws bursting in were

down. The left arm of one of the deputies still standing hung limp and bloody down one side, but he gamely fired his rifle with his one good hand, spun the weapon around the lever to jack a fresh shell into the smoking breech. An outlaw reared back, clawing at his face, hat spilling, gun dropping.

Largo squirmed, reaching for the fallen pistol and Langtry hauled back, pulling him up short. Largo's small eyes seemed to bulge as he looked back over his shoulder and then he lifted his manacled feet and drove them into Langtry's face. The rancher grunted and tasted hot blood, felt skin above his eyes split, blood blinding him briefly. He was up against Magill for a moment and then Largo hauled him bodily forward to snatch up the pistol from the floor, rolled on to his back and fired at the wounded deputy.

The man reeled off the wall, fell against one of the rescuers, taking him to his knees. He clung to the man and the outlaw's pistol rose and fell several times as he smashed it against the man's skull in an effort to break free.

Magill was moaning, but gamely trying to lift his pistol from leather. Largo twisted towards him and even though restricted by the manacles, rammed the smoking pistol barrel against Magill's temple and bared his teeth as he thumbed back the hammer.

Then Langtry swung the emptied Greener, smashing the barrels across Largo's wrist as the gun went off. He saw Magill's hair lift as the bullet passed through it and then he smashed the Greener across Largo's face. The big nose crunched and blood flowed as the killer spread out on his face, unconscious.

Langtry snatched the sixgun from the man's curled fingers, found enough slack in the chain to use the edge of his left hand to fan the hammer spur. There were only three shots left in the Colt, but two outlaws went down, one dragging himself over the bodies jamming the doorway, the other crumpling, unmoving.

Langtry spun towards the rawboned man he had picked as the leader, hurled the empty gun at him, saw it glance off the man's head.

That was it for the outlaw: everything had gone wrong. Most of his men were dead or dying, Largo was out to it and now he reeled, only semiconscious after that gun bounced off his skull.

Staggering, he lunged for the door, widened the opening with his shoulder and staggered out into the hammering rain.

The one deputy remaining on his feet, a bloody streak on one side of his face, limping with more blood showing below his right knee, lifted his rifle and blazed three fast shots after the man. Splinters flew, sparks burst from one iron hinge and then the doorway was empty, only a blurred oblong through the haze of gunsmoke.

Langtry shook his head, wiping blood from his eyes and saw that the red-haired deputy who was still standing was grinning so tight his face looked like a death's head,

'By God, we done drove 'em off, Buck! Largo's men! An' we drove 'em off — you an' me!'

★ ★ ★

The court was so crowded it seemed as if the walls would bulge outwards and spring a leak, allowing the set-in rain to come flooding inside. There was a raucous murmuring that cost Judge Augustus Le May two prime gavel-heads before he finally managed to quieten down the folks of Laredo.

There had a been a good crowd in the court-house on the corner of Fender and Front Streets earlier this day, but since the foiled rescue attempt at the jailhouse, now it seemed as if the whole blamed town had packed themselves in. Even so, the walks outside were crowded, folk standing on packing cases beneath the steamy windows in an effort to see and hear the goings-on.

Not a few of the crowd wanted to shake the hand of Buck Langtry or slap him on the back. They saw him as some kind of saviour. Cal Magill wasn't all that popular, but folk had faith in him because he did keep Laredo pretty well law-abiding and that was no easy job in this neck of the woods. Trail men, border riff-raff, men on the dodge making for the outlaw country beyond town — Magill took them all on and bent them to his way or threw them in jail. So he had been known to take the odd bribe . . . well, the job didn't pay much and as long as he was discreet about it folk were willing to go along. They might elect themselves a more honest sheriff, but they didn't know a tougher one who would do the kind of job Magill did. So Langtry saving the man's neck — *when he didn't have to*, at that! — just had to be a big plus for the town and for Langtry himself.

A bunch of townsfolk made that quite clear to Judge Le May.

The judge was a thick-necked man,

not unhandsome even though his jowls seemed a mite loose and there was a network of red-and-blue veins in a fairly large nose. He knew he could do only one thing right now.

The jurors had already spelled it out that no matter what evidence was produced and deliberated on in this court this day, they would bring in only a 'not guilty' verdict in favour of Buck Langtry.

Hell, how could any Laredo man do otherwise? He had not only saved the life of their sheriff, but he had foiled the atttempt to break-out that killer Largo and have him on the loose again.

'Judge, if that ain't the most god-damnedest civic-mindedness we ever seen, then we dunno what is. An' any man who thinks different had best start packin' and move outa this town because his life won't be worth livin' if he's loco enough to try an' stay on . . . '

That was how it was put to Augustus Le May and, fact was, he had always liked Buck Langtry anyway and didn't much care for high-and-mighty Mitch Tyrell and his M.C.V. Cattlemen's Association.

Not that he felt like going along with the town right now: he was still knocked seven ways to Sunday by the way Ginger had reacted in San Antone and he would have liked nothing better than to vent his spleen on anything within reach. But, no, Buck Langtry had earned leniency and, anyway, there was still that son of a bitch Largo to deal with and he could work himself up into a fine old state before they brought the man before him.

So, no one in that steamy, smoky, tense court room was surprised when the judge announced that 'because of the civic-mindedness and selflessness and plain damn courage of Buck Langtry, all charges were hereby dropped — and any man who might consider finding new charges had best have enough gumption to have his horse saddled and ready to run, right before he tried to bring such charges against Langtry in this town!'

The rafters rang with cheering and Langtry winced at the noise, his head bandaged. Deputy Red Satterlee, grinned widely and unlocked the handcuffs where he sat in the dock. 'Good deal, Buck! Good deal, man! You saved my neck, too.'

Langtry stood and tried to make his way to the side door, staggering under claps on the back and shouted remarks: 'Magill mayn't be our favourite man, Buck, but he is the law here an' he does a good-enough job!'

'Man, if Largo had gotten loose, he an' his bunch woulda wiped this town off the map just 'cause we locked him up here!'

'You made yourself five hundred new friends this day, Buck Langtry! You're our favourite man now!'

And then he came face-to-face with Sheriff Cal Magill, one arm in a sling, a bandage around his head, a pistol in his hand. Their gazes locked and after a moment Magill smiled slowly.

'You got my thanks, Buck.'

'So he should!' someone shouted. 'You're standing there because of Langtry, no-other reason!'

'Yeah, there is,' someone else said. 'He's got a hard head!'

That brought a laugh and for once Magill didn't scowl. He rammed his gun into his belt and gripped hands with Langtry. 'Sorry I gave you such a hard time, Buck. But, then, if I hadn't, you wouldn't've been in the jail to keep Largo from breakin' out, would you?'

Langtry smiled slowly. 'It's an ill wind, as they say, Cal.'

Then the sheriff stepped aside and took out his gun again and Langtry found himself facing Ed Largo.

The man's face was swollen and bruised, his nose heavily bandaged. There was a large gap in his front teeth and his jaw was lopisided. His piggy eyes were pinched way down to pin-points.

'You lousy bastard! I stuck up for you an' you threw me to the wolves.'

Langtry shook his head slowly. 'If you can't figure out why I couldn't let a snake like you get loose, Largo, you're more loco than I figured.'

As he pushed through the crowd the outlaw screamed behind him, his voice cracking with his hate.

'You're a dead man, Langtry! I don't care what they do to me, you're *dead*! Hear? If I can't do it someone else will. You'll never know another peaceful minute 'cause you'll never know when the bullet's comin'. Just be good and damn sure it *is* comin' — and it's got your name on it!'

Magill hustled the killer roughly into the still noisy courtroom where the sour-faced Judge Le May was waiting to throw the book at Largo: the man faced prison for the rest of his life, or, if Le May had his way, a short trip to the gallows.

Either way, Ed Largo's career was over, Augustus Le May aimed to see to that . . .

In the office of Willard S. Nevada, attorney-at-law, Mitch Tyrell fumed and strode restlessly back and forth, unmindful and uncaring that his heavy range boots were muddying-up Nevada's fancy carpet.

Swede Andersen, still shaky on his walking stick, lowered himself gingerly into a chair and adjusted the bandage swathing his face. His eyes showed clearly enough and they were burning with anger.

The attorney was pouring drinks with a shaky hand at a small side table, brought two across, handing them to the cowmen. He jumped when Tyrell slapped the glass out of his hand, liquor splashing on the front of Nevada's pearl-grey vest.

He flushed, a short man, now stretching up to his full height of five-feet-five in indignation.

'By God, you're an ill-mannered, crass man, Mitchell!'

'And you're a damn fool taking my money under false pretences!' Tyrell raged, while Swede sipped his drink awkwardly because of the bandage.

The lawyer's flush deepened. 'That's a damn lie! I had a damn good case prepared and Langtry would've had a mandatory jail sentence of at least thirty days — *if* I'd had a chance to present it!'

Mitch Tyrell curled a lip. 'Yeah, well you sure did a fine job of that, didn't you! Never opened your mouth, never so much as made a protest when that senile Le May threw the goddamn case outa the goddamn court!'

Will Nevada sighed, returned to the side table and tossed down his drink and poured another. He seemed a mite calmer when he turned to face the cowmen again.

'First, any protest I might have made wouldn't have even been *heard* in the ruckus in that courtroom. Second, I know better than to go up against Augustus Le May once he's made a

66

firm decision — and all his decisions are firm as far as he's concerned. Man, he would've crucified me! I've made mistakes in my life, Mitchell, but I hope I've learned from them. It would've been the biggest mistake I ever made to even open my mouth in that courtroom . . . hell, the whole blamed town was behind the judge, not to mention Langtry.' He shook his head vigorously. 'Any man who tried to overturn Le May's decision would be finished in this town and while working for your association is lucrative enough, from here on in, you're on your own.'

The cattlemen were shocked into silence by the attorney's obviously strong feelings about this. Nevada smiled thinly as he added, 'You opened a can of worms when you made your move on Buck Langtry, Mitchell, and now you're stuck with it. I'll forward my account within the next few days. Good-day to both of you!'

Tyrell stood by and watched sourly as Swede Andersen struggled out of the chair, not offering any help. The attorney waited, face grim, shaking a little, knowing he had taken a step he might live to regret. But, still angered by Tyrell's attitude, he waited until the cattlemen were opening the office door and then said, 'By the by, one other thing that Judge Le May ruled and notified me of, something I hadn't mentioned to you because I thought we'd be able to fight it out in court: now . . . ' He shrugged.

Tyrell glared. 'Well?'

'The Mexicans that Langtry brought across to his spread — the judge says they can work for him, help out, go where they like because they've got the right papers — as long as they don't take any pay.' Nevada smiled thinly. 'In other words, Langtry can use them to help drive his herd to Corpus Christi . . . thought you'd like to know, Mitchell.'

5

Dangerous Trails

Lester, the contract bronc-buster, had his arm in a sling when Langtry rode back into his front yard. He came out of the barn — part of which was used as a bunkhouse for Lester and the Mexicans — and waved his good arm as the rancher dismounted wearily.

'How come you're flying on one wing?' Langtry asked, off-saddling.

'Got throwed by that devil-hoss with the silver patch around his eye. Figured you had enough troubles without knowin' about my arm.'

'Gonna be all right?'

Lester smiled: that was typical of this tough-looking, though essentially easy-going rancher. First concern about the man, never mind about the unbroken horses for the remuda.

'Yeah, it'll be fine.' He moved the injured arm, grinning ruefully. 'It's the arm I've never broke before so Doc says it'll heal fast. Diego took over, saddle-broke the rest of the remuda for you.'

Langtry looked around. 'Where is he? And the others?'

'Bringin' in your herd from the canyon where they been holdin' and brandin' since they finished round-up. You've a mind, you could start trail-drivin' tomorrow.'

Buck Langtry rolled a cigarette, stuck it between Lester's thin lips and rolled one for himself. As he lit them both he saw the cook standing at the kitchen door of the cabin. The man waved the ladle he held, spat and turned back into the kitchen. Langtry smiled.

'I see Cookie's in his usual good mood.'

Lester grinned. 'Been gripin' ever since we got word they'd turned you loose. But he's made a whole slew of biscuits and soda-dodgers for the trail, been jerkin' venison and beef for a week, and had me fetch in more flour and coffee and beans. Like I said, you want to, you can start hazin' them cows north tomorrow sun-up.'

Langtry looked around the spread — the cabin and the barn, a smithy's forge, corrals, and a kind of sapling-and-bark shelter for the personal mounts for when it was raining. The skies were leaden but the rain had stopped. He kicked at the muddy ground, figuring any trail north right now would be gluey, slowing any herd.

Which would include the association's because they would have had the rain, too. By hell, he might yet be able to reach Corpus Christi before the Gulf boats sailed. There might be a little trouble getting his own herd on board but he figured he could handle that when and if it arose.

'What's the tally, Les? You know?'

'Raoul was workin' on some figures this mornin' before they rode out. He

71

reckons around three-fifty head. They picked up more mavericks than they figured on.'

Langtry whistled softly. That was good news, mighty good news. If he could sell at New Orleans prices, even after expenses, he'd have enough to clear the bank loan on the dam and a bit left over. Not much, but it would see him through the winter and then he'd go back deep into the hills and bring in wild cattle again, like last season. Bring 'em down earlier this year though, fatten them up on the dam-fed home pastures.

He shook his head, ending the dreaming. There was a lot to do if they were going to start a trail drive.

'Les, I'll give you a note to the bank to pay you for your work. 'Preciate all the hours you've put in to get me a manageable remuda.'

Lester scratched at one ear, took a final drag on his quirly and flicked away the butt, clearing his throat as he looked up at Langtry.

'Buck, I'd like to come along. On the drive.'

The rancher frowned, his eyes going to the man's injured arm.

'Oh, I won't be operatin' one-hundred-per, but I can pull my weight. I can still ride and even rope one-handed, haze hosses — *and* cows — cut-out the day's mounts and so on. Might take me a mite longer and I could need a hand saddling-up, though I can do it given the time . . . '

'Les, it's more than two hundred miles and we'll have to travel through outlaw country. No use to following the association's herds: they'll see there's no feed or water left for my cows. Can't let you take the risk, *amigo*, though I surely do 'preciate the offer.'

'Hell, Buck, what'm I gonna do? I'll mooch around while I'm waitin' for my arm to heal, drink or gamble away what you pay me . . . no one's gonna hire me while I've got my arm in a sling and there won't be no bronc-bustin' done now till next season. I come with you, I don't care if you pay me or not, but I'm ridin' with friends an' there'll be campfire talk an' larkin' around — an' I will be useful, I swear.'

Langtry held up a hand. 'Whoa! Never heard you talk so much in one bit before, Les! OK, OK — you want to come along, you can. First time you feel it's getting too much, then head for the nearest town and no hard feelings.'

Lester grinned from ear to ear, the effect spoilt some by the teeth missing from bronc-busting accidents over the years. But he sure looked happy. And, truth was, Langtry would be happy to have him along, anyway.

The rancher unshipped his coiled lariat from the saddle horn and ducked between the bars of the corral fence.

'I'll rope me a mount and ride out to see Raoul and the others. That silver-eyed devil-hoss broke now?'

Lester seemed a little unsure. 'Diego got him ridin' easy but Pancho had trouble with him.' Lester watched as the horse in question rolled the eye with the star-shaped silver-grey hair around it as he watched Langtry approach, shaking out his rope. The other horses milled about slowly but without alarm. The silver-eyed dun pawed the ground as if in challenge.

Lester stepped closer to the rails. 'I named him Squint. *Watch him, Buck!* He's a cantankerous cuss still.'

'Makes two of us . . . ' Langtry expertly backed the horse into an angle of the fence and dropped his rope over its head neatly. The horse reared and whinnied and pawed the air, then dropped the forelegs, shook its head, snorting and waited while Langtry came in hand-over-hand on the rope and stroked the quivering, arched neck.

The rancher grinned, releasing a long sigh at the same time. 'Reckon Diego's done a good job, Les.'

''Course it could be you just naturally got a way with broncs.'

Langtry continued to rub the neck and scratch the horse behind the ear, smiling. 'Yeah, could be,' he allowed.

Mitchell Tyrell leaned forward in the saddle of his big dun mare on the part of the range on his land known as Clancy's Spur. It was named after his father who had died here when horned by a wild longhorn he had brush-popped early one fall morning. They'd found the old man ten feet up in the branches of a sycamore, most of his innards dangling, amazingly still alive. But he'd died before they got him back to the ranch house and Mitchell had gone hunting that killer bull, finally spooking the animal, recognizing it from his father's dying words and the dark bloodstain still blotching one horn. He'd been out of his head with grief over his father, shot the animal through the hips, hacked its legs off with an axe and rode back to the draw where he'd left it for three days until it had finally died, half-eaten by coyotes and buzzards and crows.

He'd had nightmares for years afterwards, but he had never regretted his savagery, for he'd loved his father and he'd taken it as a slight from God Himself for allowing Clancy Tyrell to die in such a fashion.

Mitch had been fifteen years old at the time . . .

So this was a special place to him, this high crag on the spur range that commemorated his father.

From it, he could see over the north-west corner of Ripple L and his face tightened now as he watched the small herd starting out through the hogbacks towards the high trail that could take them to only one place: outlaw country.

'By hell, that son of a bitch is gonna do it!' he said aloud. 'Goddamn you, Mr Buck Langtry! Goddamn your stubbornness and your . . . your grit!' It was a reluctant compliment, but he felt he had no choice: Langtry had demonstrated his grit in the past on many occasions and this was just one more time. Right after foiling that jailbreak . . .

What bothered Mitch Tyrell most was that the man might even make it to Corpus Christi in time to get his herds on to the Gulf steamers — and he even had a shaky feeling in his gut that the lousy damn greaser-lover could even make it ahead of his own herds. For the rain had turned the regular trail to a gooey mush and he had sent a man out to see what progess the association herd had made and was mighty disappointed to learn they were held up this side of the swollen river. Four days, and they'd only reached the *river*.

The whole damn world was turning against him, of a sudden! he allowed bitterly. Every move he had made of late had been a wrong one. Now, not only had the seemingly perfect plan for cleaning-out Langtry blown-up in his face, the damn weather was working agin him, too!

The rain had turned the regular trail into a mire, but — thanks to his own planning! — Langtry had no choice but to drive *his* cows through outlaw country, *high* country, rockier than the normal trail, less prone to muddying-up and bogging-down any outfit.

Providing Langtry had no real trouble with the outlaws who swarmed through that lawless territory, the man might make it to the Gulf first — complete with his goddamned crew of greasers.

He smashed a big hand down on to his pommel, cursing at the pain that ran through his wrist, rubbing the underside of his hand vigorously.

'Well, we'll just have to see about that!' he gritted tautly, raising his field-glasses again and watching the small herd with its remuda, constantly moving riders and single chuckwagon, lumber up the trail towards the outlaw country. 'Yeah — maybe we'll just have to see about that . . . '

★ ★ ★

79

Swede Andersen was sitting on his porch when Tyrell rode in on his way back to the Double T. His father had devised that brand — two off-set Ts, one slighter higher than the other. The Tyrells, Clancy and Mitchell, well, now it was only Mitchell, but he figured he'd maybe have a son of his own one day; he wasn't yet too old or set in his ways, and then the Double T would have its true meaning again.

Andersen showed no pleasure in seeing Tyrell as the rancher clumped up on to the porch, hitched a hip over the rail and began to fill his pipe.

'Langtry's on the move. Driving his herd up through outlaw country.'

Swede arched his heavy eyebrows beneath the bandages. 'Pretty damn quick!'

Tyrell sucked and puffed at his pipe until he had it going to his satisfaction. 'Mmm. That high country won't be as boggy as the regular trail. We're still stuck at the river . . . could be Langtry'll get there ahead of us.'

'The hell you say!' Swede sat up straighter in his chair, grimacing at the pain it caused him.

'There's just a chance — unless we take steps to make sure it never happens.'

Swede glared. 'Now what you got in mind? Another great foolproof plan? Haf to tell you, Mitch, your plans don't do so good lately.'

Tyrell's eyes narrowed. 'A smart man always has a contingency plan, Swede. Look, Langtry's in outlaw country, so he has to expect trouble. All we do is make sure he gets it.'

Swede had to digest that, looked up sharply. 'How?'

Tyrell smiled. 'Well, it's natural that his herds are gonna be hit in country like that. All we gotta do is see that it happens.' Anticipating Swede's next question, Tyrell leaned forward. 'There's that feller we used once when Langtry first took up his grant and I had to move my stock out.' For a moment Tyrell allowed himself the indulgence of anger at the memory: why, the cabin Langtry was using had been one of Double T's line-shacks at the time. 'Chuckaluck, wasn't it?'

Swede nodded slowly. 'Langtry shoot him in the hip so he walk with a limp ever since.'

'Yeah. So he'll remember Langtry and he'll remember us. You and me are gonna ride up and see him.'

Swede stiffened. 'Not me. I can't ride that far in that country.'

'Sure you can — and you will. I want you in this, Swede. It's as much for your benefit as mine.'

'*I* don't want Langtry's land!'

'Goddamnit, I don't care so much about *using* the land, I just want him outa there! He's got no right to that land! It belongs to Americans and he's tainted somewhere in his past with Mexican blood. His ancestor was Spanish and had that land granted to him or *his* ancestors by some king of Spain. Well, we kicked the Spanish and the Mexes back below the Rio long ago and to my way of thinking they forfeited all rights to land in US territory. Government don't think that way but the hell with the government! I've got to live here and I want that land back in American hands. Now, you get someone to saddle you a horse, Swede. You're coming with me ... and if Chuckaluck won't play along, we'll stampede Langtry's herd ourselves. Outlaws'll be blamed, anyway.'

Swede was a hard man, but something had happened to him after the beating Langtry had given him in the jail. However, he didn't want to argue with Mitch Tyrell when the man was in this kind of mood: he was kind of loco when on the subject of old Spanish land grants and Buck Langtry.

'All right, I come. But you ride a dangerous trail, Mitch.'

Tyrell smiled crookedly. 'Not just me, amigo. One day this whole part of Texas'll thank me for what I'm doing.'

Yes. Even slow-thinking Swede Andersen could see that Mitch Tyrell had his sights set higher than just a few hundred acres of semi-barren land tucked away in a remote part of the border country.

★ ★ ★

The man called Chuckaluck was swarthy, blackbearded, had hair hanging to his shoulders, and wore clothing that had more patches than original cloth. But his guns were oiled and cleaned and ready for action.

He was just under six feet, hard-bitten and suspicious of Mitch Tyrell.

The two ranchers were uneasy under the cold stare of Chuckaluck and the other five outlaws gathered outside the old weathered shack in this hidden canyon.

Tyrell saw that two of the men were nursing wounds covered by dirty bandages. Somehow, given the kind of life these men led, he knew he shouldn't have been surprised.

'You better have a good reason for

comin' up here, Tyrell,' Chuckaluck said in his gravelly voice.

Mitch Tyrell tried to appear relaxed, although he was far from it. 'I figure you're a man smart enough to listen to a proposition that'll turn you a nice profit.'

The outlaw sniffed and glanced again at the Swede, then Tyrell. 'Well, now, that depends on the proposition, don't it? And how much profit there's to be made.'

'Well, s'pose you were told how to pick yourself up around three hundred cows — and had a guaranteed buyer for 'em? Not a man who'd pay the usual cheap, rustled stock rates, but market price . . . just like a legitimate sale.'

The whole bunch of outlaws were showing interest now, though a couple were having a little trouble figuring out what was going on.

'Sounds like a good enough deal,' Chuckaluck allowed slowly. ''Course, I wouldn't spect to *pick up* these cows easy-like, without some sort of risk — '

'Minimal,' the rancher assured him. 'The cattle are already in country you know as well as your own name and there are only six Mexicans and two whites with them; one of the whites even has a busted arm.'

Chuckaluck was showing real interest now and he swung his gaze back to Mitch Tyrell. 'I s'pose it don't matter if the white men get caught in any shootin' . . . ?'

Mitch smiled. 'It would make a lot of men in Melody Creek Valley very happy if they were, Chuckaluck . . . I don't care about the greasers one way or the other.'

The outlaw nodded slightly. 'They ain't a problem. Sounds important to you to get rid of these white men, though. Maybe only one . . . huh?'

Mitch didn't like the way it was going but had to answer. 'Yes — Buck Langtry.'

Chuckaluck leaned forward swiftly.

'Langtry? Now there's a name that makes a kinda music for me.' He glanced around at his men, his dark eyes sparking now. 'You likely recollect him an' me had a difficulty once. We traded a little lead when he first moved in here and he put a shot into my hip. Damaged the nerves clear down my leg into my foot. No way of fixin' it and it gives me pure Kentucky hell every time it rains or it gets cold. Oh, you don't have no more worries about Mr Buck Langtry, Tyrell. If he's in my country, then this is where he's gonna be buried . . . but I'll thank you for double market price on the cows.'

The outlaws chuckled at Chuckaluck's smart move and Tyrell flushed, started to protest, but when a gun hammer clicked somewhere close by, he swiftly held up a hand and nodded.

'Had me a notion you might even do the job for nothin' there for a moment,' he said ruefully, and Chuckaluck laughed outright.

'Nope. If I can make me a fast buck or two outa Langtry, then I aims to — but I got me another chore I have to do first.'

'No. This has to take priority.'

Chuckaluck smiled crookedly as he shook his head. 'Oh, no it don't. I'm already in plenty bad with Ed Largo.' He gestured to the two men with the dirty bandages. 'We kinda got squeezed out again by that goddamn Langtry! — when we tried to get Ed free before.'

The ranchers both showed their surprise. 'That was you?' asked Mitch Tyrell.

'Yeah. Me and Ed go back a'ways. He had one of his old hands, name of Bart Venters, hire us to get him out. We gotta make one more try or none of us is gonna be sleepin' too good for the next few years. So, I get that outa the way and me and th' boys'll gladly take care of Langtry. Take it or leave it, Tyrell.'

The rancher was angry. 'You're afraid of Largo!'

'Damn right! Any man who ain't is a fool bent on suicide. Now, which is it to be? You wanna wait or go take care of your own troubles?'

6

Dead Men

Chuckaluck decided to do the rescue job alone.

He had had several run-ins with Sheriff Cal Magill over the years but mostly over a little wide-looping; once or twice over a shooting that Magill couldn't quite lay at Chuckaluck's feet.

He was a wanted man in several states, had some train hold-ups and one bank robbery on his crime sheet and the rewards totalled a couple of thousand dollars. It would seem that Chuckaluck wasn't a real bad-ass outlaw, but that was only because not all of his crimes had come to the attention of the law.

He was a killer when he was riled, and had accounted for at least eleven men over the years. Sober, he could control his anger, but with a few red-eyes under his belt, he was likely to go berserk if something upset him. And if there was a woman handy then she suffered — badly. Amending that 'he had killed eleven men over the years' it has to be said he had also killed two women and scarred one for life. Somehow these things had never come up when Wanted dodgers were being put out on him.

So, while there was *some* risk in riding openly into Laredo, Chuckaluck figured it was worth it just to let Ed Largo see he was at least *trying* to bust him loose. He came in by the back streets and sought out a borderline sawbones, name of Longstreet. Back when Chuckaluck knew him on a more regular basis, in several border towns and a couple up in Indian Territory, Longstreet had been known amongst the outlaw fraternity as Doc Bullets, because he had removed so many from the hides of men on the dodge.

And his fees weren't exorbitant: a few

dollars and a few bottles of whiskey. It was a wonder he had lived so long, but he always had a few patients in Laredo, poor folk, mostly, and a few outlaws who still needed what skills he had left for removing lead from under their hides.

Thing is, the man was still only in his forties and yet Chuckaluck always thought of him as being old. He sure as hell looked old: seamed, sunken cheeks, rheumy eyes, colourless hair that hung lankly from his scalp, leaving plenty of naked, polished skin showing, a nicotine-stained moustache and hairy ears. His hands shook most of the time, but he could steady them up with a few drinks.

So when Chuckaluck rapped on the man's rear door and it was finally opened, he held up a bottle in each hand. It was sourmash whiskey made by Whiskey Joe Thunder, a half-breed Cherokee member of Chuckaluck's wild bunch.

Doc Bullets stood aside and deftly

relieved the outlaw of the bottles as he entered the sour-smelling house. He left the door for Chuckaluck to close, busy removing the cork from the first bottle with his teeth. He spat it on to a deal table that was stacked with dirty dishes and overflowing coffee-can lids that had been used as ashtrays. He sniffed the neck, took a swig and held it in his mouth, cheeks and eyes bulging before swallowing.

Breath exploded from him and he shook his upper body, turned to look at his visitor.

'Man, whatever your trouble is, consider it fixed! You've just paid in advance in a currency I respect.'

'You know who I am, Doc?'

Longstreet squinted, took another, smaller swig. 'Chuck-someone-or-other . . . memory's not what it used to be.'

The outlaw took the man's arm and steered him through to the room Longstreet used as an office and surgery.

'Doc, I'm still carryin' that bullet in

my hip that Buck Langtry put there a couple years back. You recollect tellin' me it could never be moved, but might work its way out? First signs would be when the scar started to open and weep, you said.'

Longstreet had a little trouble remembering but started to nod and Chuckaluck grew impatient, undoing his trouser belt after hanging his gun rig over the back of a chair.

'Well, it's started, Doc; weepin' — and it's givin' me pure hell.'

He dropped his trousers, pulled up his grimy undershirt and half-turned to show the sawbones. Doc Bullets took one more swig, wiped his mouth with the back of his hand, and leaned closer to examine the twisted scar. He took out a pair of wire-framed spectacles and put them on, peered again at the outlaw's hip, took off the glasses and wiped the lenses on a piece of cloth, readjusted and took one more look.

He frowned, glancing up at Chuckaluck. 'That scar hasn't opened up

— it's not weeping at all.'

The outlaw looked at him steadily. 'Look again, Doc. It's weepin'. Needs a big thick pad of cotton taped over it, wouldn't you reckon?'

'Well, if it really was weeping, I'd agree but . . . '

He broke off as Chuckaluck drew his gun from the holster hanging over the back of the chair. The outlaw cocked the pistol, aimed it at the bottle of whiskey the doctor had placed on the edge of a cupboard.

'You look again, Doc . . . '

Longstreet swallowed, looking at his bottle in alarm. 'Er . . . yes . . . yes, you're right. The wound is weeping and does need a pad. Perhaps I should tape it more down into the hollow of your groin . . . ?'

Chuckaluck grinned. 'Now you're gettin' the idea, Doc,' he said, uncocking the gun but not putting it away in the holster.

Sweating now, Longstreet began preparing his things.

When he came back to the outlaw, he wasn't really surprised when Chuck-aluck held out his left hand towards him.

There was a Remington over-and-under .44 calibre derringer resting on the calloused skin.

★   ★   ★

Some of the men in the Holey Dollar saloon on Mesquite Street in the red light district of Laredo recognized Chuckaluck.

He drank red-eye alone beneath the framed silver dollar with the bullet hole shot squarely through the centre: legend had it that this was done by Clay Allison after he'd shot himself in the foot and was hopping about with the aid of a flimsy crutch. Eye-witnesses claimed he hitched the heavily ban-daged foot on to a bent section of the crutch, balanced precariously on his good leg, tossed the dollar into the air and using the same hand drew his sixgun and put his bullet plumb through the centre before it came down to head level.

The proprietor was so impressed that he promised Allison free drinks for the rest of his life — figuring the half-loco gunfighter wouldn't have too long to live anyway — and changed the name of his saloon to the Holey Dollar.

It was almost a shrine that dollar, respected by even the hardcases who drank at the bar. So when Chuckaluck drew his own sixgun with a snarl and shot the hell out of the frame, all hell busted loose.

Outraged drinkers swarmed towards the outlaw and if he'd had any intention of using his gun again he'd made a bad mistake — for he had emptied it into the frame, shattering it into splinters and shards of glass, the holey dollar lost somewhere amidst the wreckage.

But he laid about him with the empty gun, cracked a couple of heads before the mob overwhelmed him and carried him to the floor where he took several brutal kicks and a slew of punches before they hauled him upright, bloody and dazed, until Cal Magill came bursting in with his sawn-off shotgun.

His eyes widened when he saw Chuckaluck. 'Judas priest, my luck's changin'! First I nail Ed Largo, now I've got Chuckaluck Magraw on the wrong end of my gun!'

The barkeep, down on his knees, scrabbling about with bleeding fingers while he looked for his holey dollar, looked up at the sheriff.

'Blame fool put away half a bottle of red-eye and without a word drew his gun and shot up my Clay Allison holey dollar — then started layin' about him.'

He gestured to four men holding bleeding or swollen heads. Magill looked at the outlaw.

'Looks to me like he was outnumbered. Well, that makes no nevermind.' He took the man's empty gun that someone handed him, rammed it into his belt and jerked the shotgun. 'Come on along nice and easy, Chuck, or you're gonna have these twin barrels bent over your thick skull.'

The outlaw spat on the sheriff's boots and the lawman rammed the butt of his shotgun into the man's spine, knocking him to his knees. He waited impatiently for the gagging man to get to his feet again, then marched him out into the night.

Ed Largo was sleeping on his bunk when the noise of the lawman bringing in Chuckaluck woke him. He half sat up, blinking in the lantern light as Magill shoved the outlaw roughly into the adjoining cell.

'Now strip down — I aim to make sure you're not carryin' any weapon.'

Chuckaluck growled and cursed his protests as he took off his grimy clothes and on the lawman's orders pushed them through the bars into the passage.

'What's that?' Magill asked sharply, seeing the newly taped pad on the outlaw's hip, running down into the groin area.

'Goddamn hip's givin' me hell. Old

wound started weepin', couldn't stand the pain no more so I come in to see a sawbones.' Chuckaluck swore savagely. 'Figured to deaden the pain some with a little red-eye, now look what's happened to me!'

He ended with a whining voice and Magill chuckled.

'Well, you're just a poor, unlucky, widdle feller, ain't you, Chucky-wucky! Well, it's worse luck than you know, 'cause I've got me a new bunch of dodgers on you and there's one for a bank hold-up in El Paso last year where two tellers were shot — by you.'

'You can't prove that!'

Magill was examining the clothes Magraw had taken off, grimaced as he pushed them back through the bars, wiping his hands down his own trousers.

'Don't you ever wash?'

'What for? Ain't no pretty women where I come from. Judas this hip's blamed sore! One of them kicks in the saloon must've landed on it.' He started to peel away Doc Bullets' tape edging the pad. 'Mebbe I better have another sawbones take a look at it, Sher'ff.'

'And mebbe you better shut up and go to sleep,' the sheriff snapped back. 'You're gonna be facin' Judge Le May come mornin'.'

'Wanna bet?'

Magill was turning away down the passage, his gun held loosely by the stock down at his side. He swung back sharply at Chuckaluck's tone and his eyes bulged when he saw the derringer the man had taken from under the taped cotton pad covering his hip and groin. He swore and started to bring up the shotgun, but the outlaw, at the bars now, fired, and the small weapon cracked like a whip in the cell block and Cal Magill reeled as the .44 calibre ball smashed into his shoulder, twisting him into the wall. He staggered, dropping his shotgun, fell to his knees just outside the bars of Ed Largo's cell.

The killer was there in an instant, reaching through, twisting his fingers in the sheriff's hair, smashing his head into the iron-work. The lawman slid down in an untidy heap, toppled sideways, his upper body outside Chuckaluck's cell now.

'Get the keys!' Largo snapped to the outlaw, who was struggling into his clothes. 'Goddamnit, forget your modesty and get the lousy keys!'

'Relax. No one in the front office and the street door's closed. No one would've heard that shot.' Chuckaluck grinned. 'Guess you figured I'd forgot you, huh?'

'Yeah, I did — been amusin' myself figurin' out ways I was gonna kill you — over about a week.'

Chuckaluck gave a false laugh. 'Langtry fouled us up that last time, I decided to do it myself this time.'

'Will you, for Chrissake, hurry *up*!'

Chuckaluck tightened his belt and knelt beside the moaning, bleeding sheriff, then reached through the bars, took the cell keys from the pocket of the man's shirt. In a few seconds he was unlocking Largo's cell and the killer shoved roughly past him, picked up the sheriff's sawn-off shotgun, rammed the muzzles against the back of the wounded lawman's head and jerked both triggers.

'Judas *priest*!' yelled Chuckaluck, jumping back as blood and gore sprayed around the passage. 'Someone might hear *that*!'

Ed Largo kicked the dead man, his eyes bleak, face a mask that plain scared the hell out of the outlaw. 'The bastard treated me like dirt. Let's get our guns.'

'Make it quick, Ed. We'd best go out the back way. I got hosses waitin' in an alley.'

Largo said nothing as they burst into the front office. He kicked in the panel of the gun cupboard door, dragged out his sixgun rig. Chuckaluck picked up his own Colt and holster. The killer took two Winchesters and tossed one to Chuckaluck.

'Grab some boxes of ammo and let's go.' He dropped the bar across the street door and they hurried back down the passage in the cell block past the sheriff's body, then went out into the night and made their way to the stinking alley where the outlaw had tethered the getaway horses.

The town was full of noise from the saloons and whorehouses in the red light district. It was doubtful if anyone had heard the shotgun discharging in the jailhouse.

Chuckaluck was limping in genuine pain now and had to make three tries before he swung up into leather. Ed Largo growled impatiently, 'Move it, for Chrissake, you goddamn cripple!'

'Bein' a . . . cripple . . . got you . . . out,' Chuckaluck gasped, finally settling into leather. 'Hey! Not that way — that takes you back into town.'

Largo's face was just discernible in reflected night light. The outlaw didn't like the look of the man.

'Now what!' he asked quietly.

'Show me that goddamn judge's house.'

'Aw, shoot, Ed, we ain't got time for this!'

'Show me that son of a bitch's house or I'll blow your good leg off!' He rammed the rifle's muzzle against Chuckaluck's right knee. He sucked in a breath audibly. 'He sentenced me to forty years in the State Pen. They were gonna ship me out in two days' time so it's lucky you made your move when you did. But you make *this* move for me! Or . . . '

'OK, OK! Judas, this is madness, Ed!' He heard the rifle hammer cock and said swiftly, 'Lemme take the lead, I'll show you. But we'll have to be quick! One of the deputies is bound to check in to the law office.'

'Not too damn quick,' Largo said tightly. 'I hear the son of a bitch has himself a young daughter . . . '

Chuckaluck groaned and reluctantly led the way back towards the lights of Laredo.

7

'Hit 'Em Hard!'

The nights on the trail were restless for both men and cows. It was a strain driving through outlaw country and, during the day, several strange riders had been spotted.

Fat little Pancho put his large, chestnut gelding alongside Langtry's star-blazed dun and said with a touch of worry, 'They watch us every foot of the way, Buck.'

'Yeah. But this is a queer kind of place, Pancho. It's outlaw country, but they've kind of divided it up amongst themselves — got territories marked out like cougars or wolves. One bunch won't trespass into another's territory — unless the pickings are mighty good — *and* they think they can get away with it.'

Pancho frowned, looking at the small group watching from the edge of a distant butte. 'Then those men — they watch us pass by, but if this is not part of their territory, they let us go?'

'That's it. Injuns do the same sometimes. But, like I say, if they figure they can get away with stepping across the line they will. Our herd might be tempting, but I think we've got too many men along for them to chance coming at us.'

The Mexican unsheathed his rifle and rested the butt on his knee. 'I think I give my gun some sun. It looks kind of pale. The fresh air will do it good, eh?'

Langtry smiled as Pancho rode back to his station. He stood in the stirrups and looked around. Mighty dangerous country here, full of dry washes and arroyos, not to mention ridges high enough to give anyone with rustling ideas the advantage.

But all they could do was keep their eyes open, post double nighthawks, keep their guns handy. No use starting anything — they would just have to keep driving, wait and see.

It was the third night when they found trouble. They had made good time despite the rough nature of the country and Raoul and Diego had scouted ahead, located water in a narrow canyon. It was a small, shallow stream, fed from some underground spring that poured out of grey rocks several feet up a rocky slope.

Around the stream, lush grass grew and also green brush. It was a good place to bed down the herd — except Langtry didn't like the high walls of the canyon being so close.

He figured it would be an easy job for some men with rifles up there to either pick off the riders or drop a few steers and spook them into stampede.

But the herd needed watering, good water, for they had travelled a day and a half without a drink. They smelled the stream in the canyon and the sweet grass, and began to lumber and bawl in excitement. Langtry signed to the

Mexicans to let them go and Cookie, with Lester on the driving seat beside him, pulled the chuckwagon aside to let the cows pass.

They crushed in through the entrance, shoulders and horns rubbing, bawling, filling the canyon with sound. Raoul had placed two men inside with rawhide whips plaited in the traditional Cordovan manner. They cracked these, urging the cows towards the stream where they spread out naturally and saved a jam-up in the narrow entrance.

The dust filled the canyon with a golden haze in the light of late afternoon and soon deep shadows crept out from the walls as the sun dropped slowly down the sky, painting it with streaks of red and lavender and glowing blue. The cows drank and stood in the stream, bawled to one another, spread out on the grass.

'They oughta settle easy tonight,' Lester said, as Langtry dismounted by the cookfire where the supper was being prepared, Cookie grumbling about the

Mexicans wanting all 'them blamed gut-burnin' chillis' in all of their food, whether it be a stew or simply a pot of beans. It sure smelled savoury and Langtry's mouth salivated as he took off his hat and blotted sweat from his forehead with his shirt sleeve.

'Good spot, all right, Les.' He tilted his head and looked around at the light-edged rim of the walls. 'Be happier if we had a lot more room to work in down here.'

Les glanced up quickly, adjusting his arm in the sling. 'Yeah. Walls are kinda close. You like, I'll sleep up there tonight and keep an eye on things.'

'Was thinking of doing that myself.'

'You get some rest, Buck. You've spent a heap more time in the saddle than in your blankets since we started. I don't sleep deep with this here arm, anyways.'

Langtry nodded. 'Obliged, Les. I'll see if Cookie'll make you a few extra biscuits to take with you.'

'Long as he don't put chillis in 'em!

He's gettin' that way he'll be stirrin' 'em into our coffee pretty soon — just by way of protest.'

Langtry grinned: it was the kind of thing old Cookie would do. He'd known him in the army, but he had been a marksman then, along with Langtry, in a sniper outfit. Then one day a Yankee ball had smacked him above the left eye, glanced off the bone and knocked him out for five days. When he came round, he couldn't hit a cow at five paces with a shotgun and had a strange urge to cook. Langtry had learned to live with his eccentricities, but Cookie sure surprised some folk at what he did with food.

Like the time they were with the same trail outfit, heading on into Cheyenne. The men complained about the beef stew they were having every night — with beefsteaks for lunch and breakfast. They were tired of beef. Cookie disappeared all one day between breakfast and supper. That night he served up a new kind of stew and the

111

men reckoned it tasted just like chicken with herbs and salt. He cooked a 'special' steak for Langtry. Later, he told the men it was a mess of rattlesnakes he'd found and killed — and he cooked them with the venom sacs and all. The salty taste turned out to be Epsom salts ... A pale and weakened crew made no more complaints about the menu of beefsteak after that.

Langtry couldn't sleep, rolled out of his blankets and saddled his dun, rode slowly around the dark canyon, checking on the nighthawks, Pedro and Luis, two of Raoul's young nephews. It was their first time in the United States and they were both excited and proud to be working cattle on a real trail drive.

They assured Langtry all was well and he could see that for himself: the herd was content, had settled quickly enough! only an occasional grunt or cough or lonely bawl coming from the dark patch where they had gathered at the edge of the grass ... which they had by now almost grazed out.

He was heading back for the chuckwagon to get a cup of coffee before turning in and trying again to get a couple of hours sleep before it was his turn to ride herd, when he heard the scream.

He snapped his head around towards the western wall where Les had spread his blankets. The canyon was dimly lit with starlight, but there was enough to show him the flailing figure that hurtled down from the rim to plunge into the rocks below with a sickening smack.

★ ★ ★

Ed Largo was free, *free* — and he couldn't quite believe it.

Hell, not only free, man, but he had squared away a couple of things and he felt mighty damn good about it. First, blowing Magill's head off — served the son of a bitch right, treating him like dirt.

Then the judge — ah, now that

turned out kind of special, what with little Miss Betsy-Anne Le May as well. Now that was a bonus he hadn't been expecting. When he'd been told that the judge had a daughter, he figured she would be some fat or skinny little thing with a face that would stop a clock. He wasn't sure why he thought that, but that was the image he had.

Instead — yeah! *instead* — she turned out to be a 19-year-old sweet-meat, with hair like spun gold, a face like an angel, and a body to make a preacher kick in the church's prize' stained-glass window. 'Course, Chuck-aluck was edgy as hell, didn't want to take time out, just said kill the lousy judge and let's hightail it. Kill the daughter, too, if you want, but do it *fast*!

Uh-uh. Where's the fun in doing something like that too quickly? Besides, he had been offended by the judge's little speech before he'd brought down the forty-year sentence on his head. The man, figuring he was safe up there behind his bench with the full weight of the law of the land backing him, had called him 'vile' and 'maniacal', a 'menace to society as we know it', an 'animal who had forfeited all right to be classed as a human being'. Man, that had *hurt* somehow, gone deep inside him and turned him inside-out. No one had ever spoken to him like that — and lived. And he didn't aim to let Le May get away with it, either.

So, when they'd busted into the judge's house, set in its lawns and gardens kept in shape by a whole team of greasers, Ed Largo figured payback time was here and he aimed to make the most of it.

He did. Poor Betsy-Anne suffered and had to be gagged so her screams wouldn't alert the town. The judge had been so shaken by what he had been forced to watch that he'd had a heart attack. But to make sure he didn't recover, Largo had worked on him with a knife for a time.

The place looked like a butcher's shop by the time they left and Chuckaluck admitted — to himself — that he had never felt so queasy about a killing as he had about these two vicious murders.

The sooner he sent Largo on his way the better . . .

That was when Largo surprised him by telling him he aimed to stay with Chuckaluck's bunch in outlaw country for a spell, hide out there from the inevitable posses that would be raised after the discovery of the bodies of the judge and his daughter.

'Besides, Langtry's place ain't far, is it?'

Chuckaluck had to admit no, it wasn't all that far from the edge of the outlaw country. But then, when they had arrived back at Chuckaluck's hideout, Bart Venters was waiting and told Largo that Langtry and some Mexicans were driving a herd of cattle through the lawless territory on their way to the Gulf port of Corpus Christi.

Chuckaluck groaned. He knew what that news meant: instead of just going after Langtry like Mitch Tyrell wanted him to do, now he would have Largo tagging along and God knew what kind of hell the crazy damn killer would want to get up to.

He soon found out. Largo took over the bunch effortlessly. There wasn't even any hesitation: it just seemed natural that a man of his reputation would be in charge. Chuckaluck swallowed this bitter pill with difficulty, but he wasn't yet ready to make any real stand against Ed Largo. He had no wish to commit suicide.

So, scouts were sent out and came back with the news that Langtry's herd was making for Knifeblade Canyon in the foothills and looked like they would bed down there for the night.

'OK, we hit it,' Largo said, after studying the greasy, creased ordnance map he had found in Chuckaluck's shack. 'Go in from the south, drive the herd into the bottleneck at the northern end, and any cows that get through, we push over the cliff beyond. We leave Langtry alive, of course.'

There was a sudden silence amongst the men gathered around the map on the table in the shack. It was Whiskey Joe Thunder, pouring some of his latest brew of white lightning into tin cups for the group, who voiced the answer to what was puzzling the others.

'Make Langtry suffer . . . kill him later.'

Largo looked at the Cherokee 'breed and smiled crookedly, raising his cup in a kind of toast. 'You got some brains, Joe . . . and this is mighty good hooch! Yeah, we leave Langtry alive, but it don't mean he has to be still walkin' around, long as he's fit enough to savvy what's happenin' to his herd — and his pards. We hit 'em hard! An' make damn sure he knows about it! Joe, gimme another refill, will you? Then, gents, we move . . . '

★ ★ ★

118

Whiskey Joe Thunder scouted ahead and brought back the news that Langtry's outfit was indeed bedded-down in Knifeblade Canyon, with double nighthawks posted, and also a man up on the western rim.

'Looks like Lester, the bronc-buster. Seen a flash of white that looked like a sling for his arm.'

Largo smiled. 'Good friend of Langtry's, this Lester, I hear — that right?'

Chuckaluck, tired of being pushed into the background, spoke up. 'Yeah — a contract wrangler, but him and Langtry go back a-ways. He coulda been paid off but decided to go with the herd.'

Largo nodded. 'Good. We'll pay Lester a visit. Rest of you get into position and don't move till you get my signal.'

'Well, what is the signal?' Chuckaluck asked and Largo smiled again.

'You'll know it when you hear it. Joe, you come with me.'

Bart Venters, a man who had been Largo's sidekick for years, frowned and Chuckaluck made a note of it: could be there was another man who felt his nose was out of joint. Might be worth remembering — two tackling Largo would be way better than going it alone, but still mighty chancy.

The Cherokee led the way on foot along the rim of the canyon, Largo walking surprisingly silently for a white man, Joe Thunder thought. Lester, foolishly, had a small fire going and was sitting cross-legged, trying to roll a cigarette one-handed, concentrating. Largo moved in behind him, gun drawn, rammed the muzzle against the back of the man's head and reached over to knock tobacco and papers out of the startled bronc-buster's hand.

'Here, lemme do that for you, feller.'

Lester fell in his hurry to jump up off the log where he sat and he stayed put when the Cherokee stepped into the glow of the fire, showing him his cocked carbine. Lester twisted his head to look at Largo, paled as he recognized him from Langtry's description, but frowned as he saw the man really was rolling him a cigarette. Largo took a twig from the fire, lit up, dragged deeply, getting a good coal, then took it from between his lips, blowing a big plume of smoke into Lester's face. As the wrangler squinted and coughed, Largo stabbed forward with the burning cigarette end and clamped a hand across Lester's mouth as the man screamed in pain, clawing at his left eye.

Joe Thunder frowned, some startled himself by the move. Largo kicked Lester in the kidneys and when he fell forward into the fire, placed a boot on the back of his head, holding him there . . .

Joe grimaced and looked away. Maybe all that moonshine hooch over the years had given him a weak stomach, although he had always figured he had a pretty tough set of guts — until he'd met Ed Largo.

Largo amused himself a little longer with Lester, dragged the moaning man to the edge of the rim, stood him up and put his arm about his sagging shoulders.

'Sorry about this, *amigo*, but I want your pard Langtry to know I ain't forgot the way he left me for the law or bent a gun barrel over my head . . . you OK?'

Lester's mangled mouth glistened with blood and the smashed lips moved, but the sound he made was unintelligible.

'Aw, hell, I thought you could speak American, *amigo*. Hey, look, there's the herd down there. Now I want you to go down and give Langtry my message, OK? What's that? Can't understand what you're sayin'. Look, tell you what, you just go on down there — you'll find some way of gettin' my message across, tellin' him what I want him to know. OK? *Gracias, amigo*. Really 'preciate this. *Adios*.'

Then he placed a hand against

Lester's spine and pushed. The man screamed all the way down and Largo turned back to the sober Cherokee, spreading his hands.

'See? Knew he'd find a way to let Langtry know I'm comin' for him. Now, in case that dumb-ass Chuck-aluck an' his pards ain't realized that's my signal to hit the herd . . . ' Largo drew his pistol and fired two shots into the air.

* * *

Langtry was already moving towards the dark shape of Lester's body when the shots crashed out, and he yanked the dun's reins, palming up his sixgun, looking up. As he did so, riders came thundering into the canyon, shooting and yelling and the herd jumped up even as the men not on nighthawk rolled out of their blankets, reaching for their rifles and boots and hats — a cowboy went nowhere without his hat. Often it was the first thing he put on in the morning, even before boots or trousers.

Guns whiplashed from the rim and although Langtry ducked instinctively in the saddle, the shots came nowhere near him. They were shooting into the herd, wounding or killing his cattle, getting the smell of blood mixed with gunsmoke, guaranteed to set any trail herd thundering into all-out stampede.

He glanced at Lester's broken body, tightened his lips and unsheathed his rifle as he spurred the dun back towards the herd and the gun battle that had developed there between the attackers and his Mexicans.

Lester would have to wait — it was obvious the man was beyond help, anyway.

The cows were moving now, bawling and kicking and jumping each other's backs in their panic, moulding into a stampede towards the narrow northern end of the canyon.

Dark riders came out of the night, guns blazing, and Langtry felt the hot wind of a bullet passing his face. He turned in the saddle, bringing the cocked rifle around one-handed, firing at the dark rider. The man reared in his stirrups and went backwards over his mount's rump. The horse ran on, cannoned into Langtry's — and saved his life.

A shotgun thundered and he heard the whisper of buckshot tearing through the night not a foot from his head. If he'd been sitting upright, it would have taken his head right off his shoulders. His rifle jerked upwards against his wrist and the shotgunner's mount went down, throwing the man. He scrambled to a crouching position, bringing up the Greener, but Langtry rammed the mount into him and, as the horse rode him into the ground, he leaned out and put a shot into the spinning shape.

The Mexicans were calling to each other in Spanish, hot, excited sounds. He saw a sombrero-wearing shape spill out of the saddle and two men rode in, shooting into the rolling body on the ground. Langtry fired, missed, levered, triggered again. One of the men reeled, veered away, an arm dangling and a gun falling.

Then a horse rammed into Langtry's dun and he was going down. He tightened his grip on his rifle, had an impression of the rider leaping his mount over the kicking, thrashing, whinnying dun, fired, but the shot was wild and his face ploughed into the dirt. He rolled and skidded and when he instinctively kicked away from the dun's hoofs, he found he had lost the rifle.

Dazed, bleeding, bright lights exploding behind his eyes like the Fourth of July, he staggered upright, swayed as he groped for his sixgun. Then a horse smashed into him from behind and he was catapulted forward, slammed into the side of a second horse, and he clawed wildly at a man's leg, holding on.

He had lost his hat and vicious fingers twisted in his long hair, yanking his head back.

'Well, howdy, Langtry! Fancy us meetin' again like this!'

Through pain-blurred vision and a roaring in his ears, Langtry recognized Ed Largo.

Then something smashed across his head with stunning force, slashed back and forth across his contorted face, and he felt himself falling a long, long way, the taste of blood in his throat.

8

Lone Lady

Langtry firmly believed he was in Hell.

Somehow he never came around fully, but the blackness surrounding him was full of screams and wails of tormented souls and from time to time there was fire. It was apparently thrust towards his face for he could actually feel the heat on his skin. The lids of his right eye were stuck together with dried blood and the other eye watered with the strain of trying to cope with double the work.

His arms and legs were constricted and his head thundered, but wherever he was he couldn't quite grasp full consciousness.

He drifted away into blackness several times. There was something icy drenching him, snapping him awake, but never enough for him to realize exactly what was happening.

There were voices and he made out some words interspersed with callous laughter, but he couldn't retain them. Maybe later he would recall everything. Right now he was in too much pain . . . almost past caring.

Then he came back from the blackness one time to find that there was a grey light around him, growing stronger, making things clearer. After a while he could see properly — and wished he was back in the impenetrable blackness. Raoul, Pancho, Diego, the nephews, Pedro, Cookie — and Lester. They were all dead, mutilated terribly, and dragged off a-ways by animals. He retched — and found that he was still bound hand and foot.

But not in the usual manner, wrists tied behind his back, ankles clamped together: he was spreadeagled on the ground, wrists and ankles bound with rawhide to stakes driven deep into the earth. He was naked, hatless, and could already feel the growing heat in the sunshine spilling into the narrow canyon.

About the same time, he felt the first ants.

Just a couple of little pin-pricks on his feet and ankles. Then seconds later the burning started and he knew he was staked-out on a fire-ants' nest. *Indians* was his first thought, then he remembered the flames being thrust towards his face, the glimpse of some crazy face, and the words . . .

'That's the last of your friends, Langtry. Oh, they're still here in the canyon. You'll find them OK — all over the place!'

Laughter that broke him out in a cold sweat just remembering how it sounded. And more ants swarmed over his body to drink at the salty liquid. Fire tingled through him from a hundred different sources . . .

'We'll be goin' now. You want your herd, just follow the trail of dead cows to the edge of the cliff — the rest're down below!' Another of those crazy laughs. The voice had hardened, grown more serious when it spoke again. 'The ants might finish you, Langtry, or you might manage to get free before they do. I don't care one way or the other. You're all through. You got *nothin'* now. I'm givin' you life for as long as you can last. But you'll be better off if you let the ants finish you. 'Cause if you do survive, I'll only come after you and next time dyin'll be l-o-n-g and *almighty* painful! I guess I'm kinda lookin' forward to that, so struggle all you want. I'll be seein' you. If not later on, then we'll meet in Hell sometime.'

A stunning blow loosened his teeth and he plunged into blackness.

Now, as he writhed under the onslaught of the ants, it all came back to him. The attack on his herd, Lester falling — or being thrown — off the cliff, riders coming out of the night, the herd running in wild stampede . . . *And it had been Largo's voice taunting him!*

He moaned and bit back a curse then

131

gave way to it, snarling every filthy oath and epithet he knew, over and over until the words tumbled over his thickening tongue and he rolled his head from side to side in pain, teeth drawing blood from his lower lip.

Suddenly, he clenched his teeth and muscles bulged as he strained against the rawhide straps, wrenching and working at the stakes. The thongs cut into his wrists. Blood made his hands slippery and skin peeled away, but he kept at it, driven frantically on by the stinging of the ants that were swarming over his entire body now.

Panting, he paused, unsure whether he had actually felt the right hand stake move a fraction or not. Fire beneath his skin sent him into another thrashing frenzy and he was forced to stop because of the pain in his wrists. He was appalled when he looked at them, blood flowing from deep gashes, edged with torn flesh. Then he roared, the animal sound echoing through Knife-blade Canyon as the ants fought each other to get at his blood . . .

The pain of their venom was excruciating and he felt his eyes bulge, his tongue swelling, as he tried to remain sane enough to work out some sort of plan instead of giving way to his body's instincts to wrench and tug and rear up, *anything* to get free of the bonds.

Through the thunder in his head — much later: he didn't know how much — he heard the sounds of hoofs, the creak of saddles, jingle of spurs, and his first thought was, God, they've come back to check on me!

But then he heard outraged voices and the crunch of gravel under running boots and someone was kneeling beside him, slashing at his bonds with a knife. Someone else raised his head and tilted a canteen against his parched lips. He gagged and spluttered and swallowed wonderfully cool liquid.

'Easy, man!' a voice warned as the canteen was wrenched from his lips. 'Slow and easy . . . '

It came back. He forced himself to swallow only a trickle at a time. He was glare-blind, could make out only hazy shapes against the heat-pulsing walls.

'Who . . . ?' he managed to gasp, but he had to say it several times before they understood.

'You're OK, Buck. It's Deputy Red Satterlee. I'm headin' a posse lookin' for that murderin' son of a bitch Ed Largo — and Chuckaluck Magraw. They done killed the sheriff, then the judge an' Betsy-Anne, his daughter. Just a kid . . . '

'He . . . was . . . here.' Langtry tried to flap a hand around. 'This . . . his . . . doin' . . . '

'Yeah, sure as hell looks like it, too. Judas, Buck, your . . . kinfolk . . . an' Les an' old Cookie. Christ, man, I've never seen anythin' like it an' I was one of the first at Little Big Horn after Custer made his last stand . . . '

After that it was all a blur. Rough hands rubbing him down with soap-like juice squeezed from amole yucca plants to neutralize the fire-ants' venom. His body was covered in red welts and hives and his joints, mouth and eyes were swelling.

'He needs more attention than this, Red,' a posseman from town said.

'What about that ranch, edge of the Topaz Breaks?' another man suggested. 'There's a woman there, she might be able to do somethin'. Otherwise we'll have to have someone take him all the way back to town an' we can't afford to lose anyone.'

Langtry learned later that there were only eight men in the posse, all volunteers, outraged by the death Ed Largo had left behind. The whole of Laredo was stunned by the crimes, but there weren't too many willing to go into the outlaw country to try and hunt down Ed Largo. Some men volunteered only to pull out when their womenfolk refused to allow them to ride with Red Satterlee.

So Red and six of his men rode out after burying and reading over the

Mexicans, Lester and old Cookie. A townsman, name of Chapman, a part-time wheelwright in his fifties, escorted the semiconscious Langtry down through the rugged country they had driven the herd over a couple of days earlier and took him to the lonely ranch at the edge of the Topaz Breaks.

Langtry had little memory of it and the next few days were mostly a haze, interspersed with vaguely remembered incidents of female hands on his stings as dressings were changed and cool cotton sheets were drawn over his naked body in the bed.

It was four days before the venom-induced fever broke and he looked around him at the sparsely furnished room with the cheesecloth curtains at the glassless window flapping lazily in a warm breeze. He cleared his throat, preparing to call out, but the throat-clearing was enough, for the door opened almost immediately and a woman entered.

He blinked, feeling the grit still under

the lids of his reddened eyes. He had to squint some because he was still sensitive to light. She was a woman in her late twenties, he judged, her fair hair worn in a bun at the back of her head, but not pulled back too severely. Her face was a mite narrow, but pleasant enough, though it was plain to see she was care-worn and work-weary. Her slim hands were roughened from work but her touch was gentle — he recollected that much clearly enough.

She didn't speak and he watched her every move as she drew back the sheet and examined the squares of clean calico soaked in some kind of unguent or grease that spotted his pale body. He craned to see and released a long sigh when he saw only myriad red marks dotting his skin. The swelling had gone down and so had the fiery look.

'I think we have it beaten, Mr Langtry. I'm Janet Jarvis, by the by, and you're at my ranch. I'm not sure that you'll remember your arrival with Mr Chapman.'

'Kind of hazy — ma'am, I'm mighty obliged to you for . . . all you've done.' As he spoke, he edged the sheet up over his lower body and she smiled. Her whole face lit up and her lavender-blue eyes crinkled at the corners.

'Mr Langtry, I had six brothers and I was the eldest child and had to take care of them after our parents died of smallpox. I've been used to seeing men's naked bodies all my life.'

He felt himself flushing, merely nodded and wouldn't meet her gaze. 'Any news from Satterlee's posse?' he asked to change the subject and her smile vanished.

'They were ambushed. Red and four others got away, all wounded one way or another, but the rest were killed by the outlaws. He still isn't sure if Largo was amongst them. Naturally, he can't hope to raise another posse and, in any case, is laid up in the Laredo Infirmary.'

Langtry nodded, not speaking. She didn't say any more, left the room and returned with a tin bowl of warm water, a cloth and some salve in a large jar.

'You should wash down when you feel able, but only dab around those bites or you may knock the tops off them. Put some of this salve on when you've finished washing and it'll help the itching. You'll be hard-put not to scratch, but you'll regret it if you do.'

He nodded. 'I've been bit by fire-ants before, but not so many as this.'

'No. I'll do your back for you, if you like. You're absolutely covered in bites there.'

He hesitated before agreeing and when she had finished he waited pointedly until she left — smiling faintly — before starting on the rest of his body. The bites were beginning to itch before he had dried himself off but the salve in the jar soothed the stinging.

He was surprised to find himself dozing off afterwards and when he woke he found a cup of coffee grown cold on the chair next to the bed with some biscuits on a plate beside it. He ate ravenously and drank the cold coffee. He called, but Janet Jarvis did not answer and he swung his legs over the side of the bed, held the sheet about his waist and stumbled to the window.

She was out in the yard, sitting in the shade of a small barn with pieces of a water pump scattered around her on a square of canvas. She seemed to be having trouble fitting a cotter pin in a spring-loaded bar.

He couldn't find his clothes at first, but went looking through the small parlour and eventually discovered them in the kitchen. They had been washed, repaired and ironed. By the time he had dressed he was dizzy and felt weak, but he poured a hot cup of coffee from the pot bubbling on the wood range, drank it down, then made his unsteady way out to the yard.

She glanced up at him curiously, but didn't speak when he dropped down beside her in the shade, took the pump handle assembly from her and with the aid of a pair of pliers had the cotter pin home in a couple of minutes. He opened the tines with the broken-bladed knife she had been using as a screwdriver and handed her the assembly.

'You don't live here alone.' He made it a statement.

'Why do you say that?'

He frowned, gestured to the rugged hills and the gnarled, rough escarpment of outlaw country rearing behind. 'That's mighty lawless country up there, ma'am, and some of the worst men in this land live there.'

'They don't bother me — well, hardly ever.'

'Which means . . . ?'

She sighed, looked at him squarely. 'Hardly ever — since I killed one of them who tried to climb into my bed one night.'

Langtry was silent for a time, studying this slim woman. 'How?'

She smiled faintly. 'I sleep with a big old Colt Dragoon under my pillow.'

Again he hesitated, then said, smiling, 'Bit uncomfortable, ain't it?'

141

Her smile widened. 'But handy. Mr Langtry, I might as well tell you; I said I had six brothers. Well, one went bad. He was forced to . . . hide.' She gestured to the escarpment. 'Up there. My husband, as I learned too late, also walked both sides of the line between law and lawlessness. He said it would be good for me to be close to Kip, my brother, here, and I believed him and . . . loved him for what I saw as his thoughtfulness. Only later did I realize that he chose this place because he saw it as a way to make some fast money. Through Kip, he got to know some outlaws from that wild country and they began rustling cattle, bringing them through here after changing their brands in amongst our own herds — and my husband would sell them with our own cows. Then, one time, the law grew suspicious at the markets and they moved in. There was a shootout and Kip was killed and my husband was wounded and later sentenced to ten years in the State Penitentiary. I was under suspicion, too, for a time, but Cal Magill finally cleared me.'

'You stayed on here, though.'

She met his gaze unflinchingly. 'Oh, yes. And why wouldn't I? This is the only home I've got. No one wanted to buy it, it being so close to outlaw country. The outlaws, of course, thought they could carry on as before, but I shot a couple, killed the man I told you about and finally they let me alone.'

'You're right handy with guns, it seems.'

'Right handy,' she agreed. 'All my brothers liked guns and so did I — I was a better shot than most of them — still am.'

'None of them came to help you?'

She sobered, shook her head. 'No.' Her voice was scarcely a whisper now. 'They . . . went their own ways, met girls, got married, raised families. They didn't care for their children to know about their aunt who lived at the edge of outlaw country and who might have been mixed-up in a rustling deal. Oh, I suppose it's unfair of me to put all the blame on to them. I refused their tentative offers of help, sure that they weren't meant to be taken seriously, and then I — well, I have something of a temper and I wrote to all of them in pretty strong terms, telling them I could manage my life from here on in quite well without their interference, thank you very much. I can be very stubborn, you see.'

He smiled and saw her stiffen and sober fast as she snapped, 'What's so funny?'

He shook his head. 'Nothing really. It's just that you still sound so mad about it.'

She held the glare a moment longer, then lowered her gaze and nodded with a crooked smile. 'Yes, mad at myself for being so foolish. But, as I said, no one wants to buy the place so I'm stuck here. Oh, I could make some quick money by agreeing to a rustling deal with the outlaws, but one of the Jarvis family in jail is more than enough in my opinion.'

'You — you're gonna wait for him?'

Her shoulders stiffened. 'I believe that's more than you need to know, Mr Langtry.'

'Yeah. I . . . I'm sorry. Didn't mean to pry . . . I reckon I'll be able to do a few light chores tomorrow, so any other repairs you need doing . . .'

'You need to regain your strength — and I believe Mr Chapman said you have a ranch back in Melody Creek Valley.'

He sobered now, the memories of his cousins and his friends slamming into his mind. 'Yeah. But it don't matter now.'

She frowned. 'That's a strange thing to say.'

'Why? I've lost six kinfolk and two mighty good friends, plus a herd of cows. I'm broke. The bank'll foreclose on my spread because I owe them payments on my dam. I'm ruined. Thanks to Ed Largo and the sons of — the men who helped him.'

'Well, what will you do?'

He looked at her bleakly and she was surprised to feel a faint shiver run down her spine.

She had never seen such awesome determination. Or hatred.

'I kind of like the idea of Ed Largo financing my future.'

It was said very casually, but not for one second did she doubt this man would do exactly as he said.

9

Ruined

Red Satterlee, now Sheriff of Laredo, was back in his law office when Buck Langtry appeared in the doorway, dusty from the long ride in from the Topaz Breaks. Red thought the man looked kind of twisted-in on himself, the old easy-going, lazy manner, gone.

He straightened awkwardly in his chair, reaching for the cane he would have to use for a spell until his leg wound healed properly and heaved to his feet with a grunt. He gave Langtry a wary glance. He had seen men like this before, seen that kind of — obsessive — look about them. It was so foreign to the loner who had been the butt of mild fun in Laredo for so many years that Red felt, briefly, disoriented.

'Doc Ferris said you'd quit the

infirmary, Red. How you doing?'

'Think I'll make it. How about yourself?'

'That Jarvis woman fixed me up good But I wouldn't be here now if it wasn't for you, Red. I'm beholden.'

They gripped hands, the sheriff swaying slightly to keep his balance. 'I was only one of the posse, Buck.'

'Well, I'm obliged. On my way to the bank, see what they're gonna do about my place. But I'd like the latest estimate of the reward on Ed Largo. *And* Chuckaluck Magraw.'

Red stiffened and had to sit down, which he did awkwardly and with a thump in Cal Magill's old chair.

He frowned, half-squinting at Langtry, who waited in easy patience. Red whistled softly. 'Judas, man, when you move, you don't do it by halves! Largo *and* Chuckaluck! Now, I ain't sayin' I wouldn't be sorry to see both them varmints sent to Hell, but, Buck you're one man. You'll have to track 'em down in country swarmin' with outlaws, any one of which'll be happy to put a bullet in your back on sight.'

'Well, I guess nothing comes easy in this life, Red. How much am I looking at?'

Satterlee sighed, opened a desk drawer and brought out some papers and Wanted dodgers. 'Got the latest dodgers here. Largo's worth . . . ' His lips moved as he shuffled through dodgers from several states relating to Largo, adding the figures. 'Hell, totals here look like close to fifteen thousand! And I know there's another dodger out on him in California that must be worth another coupla thousand. Chuckaluck, well . . . let's see now . . . Hmm, he's got more'n five thousand on his head, Buck. Judas, man, if you pull this off you'll pick up twenty thousand. But I say *if*.'

'Biggest little word around, Red. Look, I don't figure it's gonna be easy, but I need to do this. I lost a lot of fine men and they need avenging, like I need the money. Can you draw me a map of where they ambushed you?'

'I can — roughly. Shorty Hanks was doin' the scoutin' and trailin', but he stopped the first bullet. So I'll be guessin' some.'

'Guess away then, Red — I need some kinda map to follow.'

Red laboured over the crude map and Langtry grew restless. When it was finished, and he was sure he could follow it in the main, he left and went to the bank.

But there was little joy there. The banker, Whit Capstick, was noted for his cold heart and it sure hadn't thawed much since the last time Langtry had seen him.

'I have shareholders and head office to answer to, Buck,' the well-fed, cold-eyed Capstick told Langtry, sprawling at ease in his heavily furnished office. 'Can't let your debts slide on forever . . . '

'Give me a coupla months, Whit, maybe less. I ought to have enough money to pay off the dam *in full* by then.'

'One month — and it has to be in full. No part payment. I shouldn't stick my neck out this way, you know . . . '

A month — to track down two of the worst killers in the country, through territory absolutely hostile to him or any other law-abiding man . . .

He stood, nodding, not offering to shake hands and seal the deal with the banker. He knew Capstick would stand by his word, but he didn't have to admire the man.

'Guess I'd best get moving then, Whit.'

'See you in a month, Buck . . . to sign the foreclosure papers!'

The banker was chuckling when Langtry left, looking and feeling mighty grim.

It was plain ornery bad luck he had to run into Mitch Tyrell. Bad luck for Tyrell, that was.

The big rancher came wheeling out of the top saloon in Laredo at that time,

The Dancing Señorita, paused just outside the ornate batwings to light a cigar, and saw Buck Langtry coming along the walk, limping slightly, head down in thought. Mitch was in a good mood: his hardcase trail boss, Pink Hardiman, had telegraphed him that the association trail herd was now on its way across the Gulf and that beef prices in New Orleans were the highest since the war. He was feeling real mellow from a few bonded whiskies from his private bottle kept for him in the Ranchero's bar of the saloon. He stepped into Langtry's path and the rancher had to stop suddenly, take a quick sidestep in order to avoid a collision. He did not look amused when he glanced up.

In fact, he barely hid a scowl and his words were clipped as he nodded curtly. 'Howdy, Mitch.'

'Good-day to you, Buck. Hear you had some bad luck, *very* bad luck, with your herd and those kinfolk of yours.' Tyrell made his face sober and shook his head. 'As you know, I have little use for . . . Mexicans, but . . . well, no man deserves to die the way they did. Nor your white friends.'

Langtry nodded very slightly and made to step around Tyrell, but the big association man couldn't let him go without at least a little crowing.

'Association herds are on the ferries now, Buck, heading for New Orleans and exceptionally high beef prices. Guess you'll be wishing you'd thrown in with us.'

Langtry seemed to think about it, spoke in that lazy drawl of his. 'No, not really, Mitch. I've an idea there wouldn't have been room for my herd on those ferries, or, if there was, some would've been lost on the way across the Gulf.'

Tyrell's eyes narrowed and he felt his mellow mood draining away slowly. 'That's not the way the association operates, Buck.'

Langtry shrugged. 'Hardly matters anyway, Mitch. *Adios*.'

He stopped in his move past Tyrell as the man's hand grasped his arm. 'Don't be in such a hurry, Buck. Look, I'm confident of selling at top price in New Orleans, and I'm feeling — expansive. I can offer more for that portion of your land I'm interested in — say another ten dollars an acre? Give you a nice little nest-egg and you can cover your arrears on the dam loan . . . '

'No, thanks, Mitch.'

Tyrell frowned. 'The hell's wrong with you, Buck? I'm offering you a sure thing! More than enough to keep the bank off your back. Christ, man, you'll make a profit on land you don't even *use*!'

Langtry smiled thinly. Tyrell was bristling now. 'A damn genuine offer and you throw it back in my face!'

'That's what I'm doing, Mitch. I guess I have to spell it out for you: you ain't never going to get any of my land. Can you savvy that?'

Mitch Tyrell's face coloured deeply and his voice rose.

'You're a damned ingrate, Buck! And you're insulting with it!'

Langtry drifted his slow gaze over Mitch Tyrell and looked deep into the man's raging eyes. 'Learn to live with it, Mitch. Now, I've nothing more to say to you so step aside.'

That did it. The rancher deliberately set himself firmly. Sighing, Langtry made to step around Mitch Tyrell and the rancher suddenly stabbed out with his burning cigar end and twisted it against the side of Langtry's neck above his frayed shirt collar. Langtry grunted and leapt wildly with pain, clapping a hand to the blister already rising on his skin. Mitch Tyrell brought over a curving right that slammed against the side of Langtry's jaw, knocked him stumbling off the boardwalk. His feet scrabbled for grip in the eroded, sloppy gutter, couldn't make it, and he fell sprawling. Men started towards them, hurrying when they realized just who the combatants were: Laredo had been waiting for years for a real clash between Langtry and Tyrell.

Mitch was a mite startled at what he had done, but then his simmering temper boiled over and he jumped down into the street beside the dazed Langtry, kicked him in the side. Langtry rolled away, kept rolling until he was clear and thrust to his feet. Tyrell moved fast for a big man, came in with a cougar-like grace, hard knuckles battering Langtry's midriff. Buck staggered back, one leg twisting, and put down a hand to keep from falling. Tyrell kicked the arm from under him and he sprawled. He rolled in towards the association man as Tyrell stomped at his head, grabbed the man's legs below the knees and heaved. Mitch staggered, flailed in an effort to keep balance, thudded to the street.

Langtry hurled himself on top of Mitch, driving a knee into the man's belly, smelling the fine bonded bourbon as breath gusted out of Tyrell. He butted Mitch in the face, grabbed his ears and smashed his head on to the street several times.

As he thrust back, rising, he was aware of the shouts of the jostling crowd that had formed a rough circle about them. Wiping blood from his nostrils and mouth, Langtry let Tyrell get halfway to his feet and lunged in, both fists swinging. The right took Tyrell under the left ear. The left fist opened a split in his right cheek, turning his head back in time for the right to crack alongside his jaw. Tyrell staggered, fighting to stay on his feet.

Langtry hooked a leg from under him and Tyrell sat down with a thump. He scooped up a handful of gravel and tossed it at Langtry's face. The rancher covered, felt pebbles sting the arm across his eyes, then closed as Tyrell came all the way up, roaring. Mitch was swinging hard, bulling in fast, taking punishment without flinching, forcing Langtry to back-pedal.

He felt the hitch rail behind him, horses either side of him whinnying and banging against him as they jerked at

157

knotted reins. Tyrell came on, bloody face wild, his blazing eyes unseeing, intent only on battering Langtry into submission.

Buck dropped to his knees as Tyrell swung, ducked out under the belly of a stomping horse, shoulder-rolling and coming up swiftly. Mitch had stumbled when the swing missed, was momentarily crushed between the two mounts, floundered over the hickory and fell flat on his back between the rail and the gutter.

He bounced up in time to meet Langtry's attack, covered his head and body with fists and elbows, taking hard blows that he knew would leave his forearms black and blue, backing-up, getting away from the hitch rail and out into the street again.

Here, he suddenly stopped and, as Langtry lunged forward, ducked under the blow and ripped a fist into the man's midriff. Langtry gagged and doubled up. Tyrell bared his teeth in triumph as he moved in, certain-sure of victory now, raising a hand to club a hammerblow on to the back of the other's neck. But Buck Langtry, despite his pain, butted him in the belly and Tyrell staggered, his blow only glancing off the rancher's shoulder. Grimacing with the effort, Buck Langtry straightened, poked three straight lefts into the middle of Tyrell's startled, blood-streaked face, snapping his head back with each blow. Then the right came whistling in and spread Tyrell's nose all over his face. Langtry moved in, Tyrell came hurtling upright and the top of his head just missed the other's battered face.

But Mitch *did* miss and he clawed wildly at this unstoppable loner — to keep from falling. Langtry was fast as a hungry mountain lion pouncing on a crippled calf. Both fists blurred as they hammered at Mitch's midriff, driving him back and back up the middle of the street now, the circle of the crowd opening out, shouting men following as Langtry kept up that relentless barrage

159

of blows. Mitch Tyrell's thick legs began to shake and weave and his efforts at protecting himself were pathetic now. His arms swayed ineffectually and when they dropped, Langtry slammed head blows through the opening; when they lifted to cover his head, Langtry battered his exposed tender midriff.

Tyrell went down on one knee suddenly. Langtry cannoned into him and Mitch grabbed at his legs, but not before a knee had smashed up under his jaw. His grip was feeble as he swayed and the way he got his hands fluttering in front of his face, not even forming fists, it looked like he was cowering.

Langtry twisted his fingers in the man's thick brown hair, jerked his head back, then abruptly forward, lifting a knee at the same time. Face and hard bone met with a crunch.

The crowd went silent. Mitch hurtled back, arms flailing, unconscious even before he sprawled in the dust, crucifix-like, bloody and defeated.

Langtry swayed on his feet, gasping for breath. He stumbled towards the nearest awning post outside the general store, wrapped his aching arms around it and, as his shaking legs gave way, slid slowly down to sit on the gritty boards of the walk.

Then he lay back with a moaning sigh, spread his arms, and let the warm sun beat down on his battered face.

* * *

Swede Andersen, his bandages removed now but his face still bruised and misshapen, sat on the straightback chair in the infirmary and looked at Mitch Tyrell propped up in the bed.

The man was heavily bandaged, his jaw bruised and grossly swollen. The sawbones had told him to avoid talking but the battered rancher was still so blazingly angry that he simply couldn't *stop* trying to talk, even though his words were slurred and difficult to understand.

'Gonna . . . kill him . . . Swede!'

'Not a good idea to try, Mitch. Langtry's tough,' Andersen told him in his quiet, thick voice. 'Look at my face — yours will be worse. Doc Ferris say you better stay put.'

Tyrell growled like a bad-tempered dog, eyes blazing through the bandages. 'Gonna . . . fix . . . him!' he said stubbornly.

Swede hesitated then said, 'I think he *too* tough for us.'

He felt uncomfortable saying it, but he had been in a strange mood since that brutal beating in the jailhouse. Never afraid of anything or anyone in an adventurous life, he was now experiencing something mighty upsetting: the thought of ever going up against Buck Langtry again scared the hell out of him.

'You shut up!' Those words were plain enough even though gritted through Tyrell's chipped teeth. 'He made a fool of me . . . humiliated me . . . in front of the whole town . . . *me!*'

His breathing became heavy, like that of a locomotive waiting to pull out of the siding with a long line of freight cars. He lifted a battered, swollen hand.

'Not gonna . . . gerraway . . . wi' . . . it! *Not!*'

'Well, he will for a while yet, Mitch. You can't do nothin' about him right now.'

Tyrell glared back so hotly that the Swede frowned and looked away: the man's eyes were positively maniacal with hate for Langtry.

★   ★   ★

By the time Langtry rode into his ranch yard, it was late afternoon and he was ready to tumble from the saddle and straight into his bunk. He had had a cut above his eye stitched up and his broken nose reset before he left town, but figured he could deal with his other injuries himself. He just wanted to clear Laredo, get back to Ripple L, having an uneasy feeling about it.

163

But the ranch was deserted and untouched as far as he could see and he turned his star-blazed dun into the corral, lugged his warbag into the cabin and flopped on to his bunk, asleep almost instantly.

★   ★   ★

The night was torn apart by a series of explosions, almost running together, at least six blasts. Fire and earth and logs erupted towards the stars and when they finally crashed back to earth, they made splashing sounds.

Langtry came awake when he heard the distant explosions and for a few moments he thought he was back at Gettysburg and the Yankee artillery had found their hiding place.

But the trembling of the cabin was only momentary and in the darkness he remembered the battering, bruising fight — every inch of his body remembered it.

He groaned as he stiffly swung his

legs over the side of the bunk, still trying to figure out what the hell was going on.

He groped his way along the wall to the door, shaking his head in an effort to clear it of the roaring sound that seemed to fill it.

But the sound came from outside his head as he soon saw when he swung back the door.

It came from a two-feet high wall of muddy water sweeping across his yard, already rising against the shaky sides of his small barn, built from clapboards and planks.

As he stumbled towards the corral so as to release the horse, he thought, *Christ! They've blown the dam!*

Then he was splashing knee-deep in the first swirl of the muddy water as he hurtled down the corral rails and lurched back as the wild-eyed dun raced for the opening. It cost him plenty in pain, but he snatched at the flying mane and leapt on to its back, using knees and curses to turn the weary animal towards the rise behind the cabin.

The water came surging in and the dun whinnied in protest as branches and debris brushed against its legs. The barn was gone, crumpling now under the onslaught and he wondered if the slight rise in the ground to where the cabin stood would slow the flood any.

Not that it mattered much. Main thing now was to get out of this alive.

The flood came surging after the fleeing horse, rising up the slope, filling the cabin now. It was built of logs, much more solid than the barn, but he reckoned it likely wouldn't stand for long if the waters kept coming at this force.

The dun was labouring but he made it to the top of the rise. He stopped the panting animal, turning it, and stared back and down. The yard was full of muddy water and debris booming hollowly against the cabin walls which were still standing. The corrals and barn were gone as was the smithy and forge. The buckboard was splintered and what remained of it floated with the other debris. The level of water climbed slowly up the slope but he could see that it was slowing and wouldn't reach to where he and the dun waited.

Well, that was the end of his dam. But he still had the debt to pay back to the bank.

Buck hadn't thought anything worse could happen to him after losing his friends and the herd. But he had underestimated that son of a bitch, Ed Largo. It had to have been him. Timed it nicely. Waited until he had arrived back at the doomed spread, then blew the dam and finished the job.

It only served to make him more impatient than ever to get on the man's trail and put a bullet in him.

10

The Guide

Janet Jarvis stood on the porch of her small ranch house and watched the rider coming in across the flats. She held an old Henry repeater, the brass receiver dulled with disuse, and she levered a shell into the breech, not recognizing her visitor.

The big old cap-and-ball Dragoon pistol was rammed into a narrow leather belt encompassing her slim waist. Then she frowned as the man came closer: looked to her like that horse didn't have a saddle, but the rider was resting a heavy rifle on his knee. There was mud halfway up the mount's legs, too.

She brought the Henry around to cradle it in her arm in such a way that she could get it shooting in an instant, and then she recognized the dishevelled figure. Buck Langtry.

He slowed the star-blazed dun as he approached the house and saw she was armed and waiting, remembering the stories she had told him about shooting outlaws who pestered her, killing one man ... Langtry jumped down from the dun, carrying his heavy rifle out to one side, lifting the other hand well away from his holstered sixgun. His boots were muddy.

'Afternoon, ma'am. Din' mean to startle you.'

'You didn't, Mr Langtry. I'm just naturally cautious.'

'A good way to be out here. I've had me something of a difficulty.'

'Your face tells me that — and no saddle or bridle.'

He nodded. 'Lost just about everything in a flood.'

Janet frowned, glanced automatically at the cloudless blue sky. 'We've had no rain here.'

'Wasn't rain. Someone blasted my

dam and water flooded my spread. Everything is under a couple of feet of mud or it's been washed away.'

She nodded pointedly at the big rifle he held. 'Not quite everything.'

He smiled. 'No. This I kept up in the rafters of my cabin, together with the shells for it.'

'It looks too big for a saddle gun.'

'Yeah, but I carried it in a canvas case strapped to my saddle under my left leg when I was hunting buffalo for a living.'

'That's a Sharps?'

'The Big-Fifty. About as powerful as you can get. Fifty-seven calibre, two-and-three-quarter-inch shells, kicks like a mule and can belt you back through a plank wall if you don't shoot right.'

She seemed interested. 'But you know how to shoot it right?'

'I was a sharp-shooter during the war at one stage, went out hunting buff afterwards and Squawman Hackett himself taught me how to make every shot count . . . and always to keep one

170

bullet for yourself if attacked by Indians.'

She didn't say anything for a moment, then lowered the Henry and turned back into the house, inviting him inside with a casual word over her shoulder.

Over coffee and sowbelly and fried eggs which she cooked up for him, Langtry told her about his troubles. She listened without interruption and when he finished and rolled himself a cigarette, she reached out for his sack of Bull Durham and the yellow wheat-straw papers and rolled a smoke for herself. She smiled and grabbed his hand while he was lighting his cigarette and lit up, blowing smoke up at an angle.

'Six brothers taught me some of little boys' bad habits — I don't smoke often, just occasionally. Do I shock you?'

'Surprise me, mebbe, not shock.'

Her smile widened, then faded slowly. 'You have your problems, Mr

Langtry. Tyrell, Largo and Chuck-aluck . . . '

'Call me Buck. Yeah, I have. I got no right to bring 'em to you — I'm already beholden to you — but I didn't want to go back into town so I cut over the range and down through the Breaks so's I wouldn't be seen by anyone watching my place.'

She drew on her cigarette and stared at the glowing end before looking directly at him. 'And what do you want from me?'

'Loan of a saddle, a carbine, shells, some grub, and a spare mount. I gotta tell you now, I've got about seventy-three cents in my pocket and that's all the cash I have in the world. But I stand by my word and I'll pay you whatever you ask and return your spare mount and gear soon as I . . . do what I'm setting out to do.'

'You're going after the reward on Largo.'

He arched his eyebrows, surprised she was so quick at picking up on his intentions. He nodded. 'And Chuck-aluck Magraw.'

Her mouth tightened. 'Yes, Chuck-aluck. I winged him once when he came prowling around here and he shot my best mare as he was leaving in return. He promised that one day he'd come back. For me . . . I'd be happy to see Chuckaluck Magraw put in jail — or shot dead.'

He couldn't help smiling a little. 'Tough l'il lady, ain't you?'

She chose to ignore that. 'You're taking on a very dangerous chore, Mr — Buck Langtry.'

He shrugged. 'Got to be done.'

Her eyes narrowed. 'But not, prima-rily, for the money. With you, revenge is the most important thing, isn't it?'

'Not so much revenge as — well, my kinfolk and my friends deserve to have justice brought to their killers. But don't get the notion I'm all noble, ma'am; I need that reward money to survive.'

'Of course, and it's only fair and

proper that Largo and Magraw who helped destroy your life should also help put it together again . . . ' She paused, smoked a little, continued to stare at him. 'How do you feel about sharing that reward money?'

Langtry frowned, trying to hide his surprise. 'I ain't greedy. Half is all I need. But share . . . ? Who with?'

'Me, of course.' He started to speak, but she held up a hand right away. 'I know that country better than you. I visited with Kip when he lived up there amongst the outlaws. Several times. You said the map that Sheriff Satterlee drew you is pretty vague, well, I know that place where he was ambushed — I can save you a lot of time.'

He was shaking his head while she was speaking, but she finished what she had to say before giving him a chance to reply.

'No. Sorry, but that's out. I don't want the problem of looking out for you as well as myself in strange country.'

'Are you deaf or is it just that you

don't pay attention?' she snapped. 'I just got through telling you I know the country, can lead you to some of the hideouts. You'll find Largo and Magraw a lot faster with me guiding you.'

'Mebbe so, but I can't do it. Hell, if something happened to you in there . . .'

'It would be my own fault entirely. I'm volunteering, Buck! No one's forcing me to go.'

Again he shook his head. 'Can't take the responsibility.'

She stabbed out her cigarette on the edge of the deal table and flicked it into the wood range. Dusting off her hands, she looked at him soberly.

'Then I'll go in there on my own — and I guarantee I'll find Largo before you do . . . and there'll be no sharing of the reward if I do.'

She was surprised when he suddenly laughed. 'You're a damn little witch, ain't you? I'll bet your husband was glad to go to jail just to get a rest from you!'

At first he thought she was going to hurl his tin plate and eating utensils at him, but then a slow crooked smile crept across her mouth.

'I can be stubborn. I told you that before . . . but you've shown me a way I can get out of this place. With that reward — even half will suit me. And you already said half is enough for you.'

He sighed. 'Miz Jarvis, I've never met a gal like you before . . . I reckon you got me beat at every turn. Well, if it'll help you out, help you get another place set up for when your husband comes outa jail . . . OK. But I still don't feel right about it — so when I tell you to keep your head down or to vamoose, you blame well do it! I want your word.'

She gave him a wide-eyed innocent look. 'Why, of course! I'll do whatever you say, Buck Langtry.'

Somehow he didn't feel too sure about that.

★   ★   ★

She knew the country all right — quite a bit better than he expected.

They started out after dark, in case anyone was watching. Langtry felt he was getting paranoid, but there was something nagging at him, something that told him things weren't just the way they seemed.

Neither with the girl nor with his spread . . .

'Why don't you sell some of your land to Mitch Tyrell?' she asked, when they stopped to water the horses at a hidden spring she led him to in a sand-floored canyon.

'Don't like him. He's got it in for Mexicans for one thing and I've got a touch of Spanish blood somewhere. My ancestor, Don Diego de la Vega Corrientes, was a Castilian, so I guess some of their stubbornness and pride has rubbed off on me a mite. Anyway, he was granted that land by the King of Spain at the time, but Don Diego had to fight Indians and twisters and floods and the rest of it to tame it. It didn't just land in his lap, all ready to raise beef. Over the years, his descendants have had their share of troubles and spilled their blood on that land, so I wouldn't feel right about letting someone like Mitch Tyrell have any part of it.'

'He's unworthy,' she commented, and he nodded.

'I guess that's what I mean. I'll give the land away to nesters if I have to, or I'll build another dam and flood it. But whatever I do with it, it'll be my decision and I won't be pushed into anything.'

He caught the flash of her teeth in reflected starlight. 'And you think *I'm* stubborn!'

He smiled. 'Yeah, I do.'

She laughed lightly. 'We'd best move on.'

She swung up into saddle, folded her hands on the horn and waited for him to mount, too. She was wearing denim pants and a checked shirt with a calfskin vest over it. Her hair had been tucked up beneath her broad-brimmed hat. She might look like a slim man from a distance, but Langtry kind of doubted it, with the way her hips flared . . .

As he lifted the reins of the spare mount, she turned her horse, leading her spare, riding alongside him. They rode on through the night, climbing into the heart of the outlaw country. It was a slow, tense, silent ride. Neither had anything to say so they held their tongues. The horses snorted occasionally as they came to a particularly steep section of trail, the saddles creaked, and the packs rubbed raspingly against their ropes. Once in a while, a stone clattered over the edge of the trail, reminding them how narrow it was and how high they were.

Langtry was mighty weary, but he daren't give in to the tiredness and doze here. Once she hissed and crouched low over her mount's neck as she hauled back on the reins suddenly.

He stopped the dun abruptly, waiting, also lying low along the horse's back. He didn't query why the sudden manoeuvre: she would have her reasons. And as he waited, he heard a faint, rasping sound, above and slightly ahead, and it took him a few moments to realize it was a man hawking and spitting.

'Guard,' she whispered. 'We angle down here . . . very slow. Try not to make any sound at all.'

She led the way, dismounting, holding her horse's bridle, whispering comfortingly into its ear. As her pack mount followed, Langtry, too, dismounted and spoke soothingly to the dun as he descended cautiously on the slope he could barely make out.

He imagined all kinds of shapes formed by the shadows and twice he actually dropped his hand to his sixgun before he realized it was just the dim light and the movement. Then she swung upwards again and stopped dead when her pack horse stumbled. They froze and stayed that way for a long five minutes, ears straining for any sounds above that would tell them they had been heard. But there was no alarm and then she led the way around a bulge of rock on a trail barely wide enough to take a horse. They mounted before they used this trail, clinging to the outward bulge.

Then abruptly the trail widened and levelled and within the hour she led him into a small canyon, halted on a rise and pointed.

'Can you see it against the stars — the pass?'

He could just make it out. 'That where they bushwhacked Red and the posse?'

'I'm sure of it. We'll wait until daylight before we move through and then, if I'm right, we climb very steeply and come to a broken ridge. Behind it lies Chuckaluck's hideout.'

'They must've trusted you — to let you ride into their hideout.'

She hesitated. 'No. I followed Kip

and my husband once. Never said anything about it . . . but I thought it wouldn't hurt to know exactly where they were hiding out.'

He glanced at her, just able to make out her face in the dim light. 'You took a mighty big chance. If you'd been spotted . . . '

'I wasn't. Now, at long last, I've been able to make use of the knowledge.'

'Well, we're here — or almost,' he allowed quietly. 'But we ain't got our hands on that money yet.'

She fell silent.

★ ★ ★

They were in position on high ground that overlooked the outlaws' valley by the time the sun came up and painted the hills with a soft gold light.

Shadows had a feathery look to them and she watched silently as Langtry unshipped the heavy Sharps, taking a U-shaped rest with a long spike of wire from where it had been taped to the gun. He drove this into the ground, wrapped a piece of gun-oil-smelling rag around the 'U' and rested the sixteen pound rifle's fore-end on the rag pad.

'Why bother with the rag?' she asked, genuinely interested.

He continued to work the gun into the position he wanted for a moment and then laid out his brass shells on a square of oily canvas. 'It helps take some of the shock, stops the fore-end jumping so much each time I shoot. Squawman taught me the trick. When the barrel gets too hot we usually . . . urinate down it, but I think we can spare water from the canteen today.'

She met his gaze soberly. 'Is the barrel going to get hot?'

He shrugged. 'Haven't fired the gun in years. I've cleaned it, but the sight could've had a knock, might throw off my aim. Once I shoot to find out, I'll wake the whole outfit down there. So I'll have to sight-in as I go along.'

'Go along doing . . . what?'

His eyes didn't waver. 'Picking off

Chuckaluck and his men.'

He heard a slight intake of her breath. She started to speak, then seemed to change her mind and nodded slowly. 'Yes, I guess that makes sense. Just for a moment I was being foolish and thinking maybe they should have some kind of warning. Forgive me — I'm new to this.'

'Janet — you can leave. I can hole-up here and pick 'em off one by one soon as they poke their heads up from that cave and the shack or anywhere else they move down there. This is a sniper's dream, this ridge, gives the best possible field of fire. You can go back down to that canyon where we watered the hosses last night . . . '

'Oh, stop wasting your breath!' she snapped, levering a shell into the Henry. 'I'm here to watch your back, so . . . get on with it!'

The outlaws were moving about now and that surprised Langtry some: his experience with men on the dodge in what they figured was a safe hideout told him that normally such men were lazy, stayed in their blankets until the sun was high or they felt like stirring.

He looked around carefully in a slow, studying sweep, but there didn't seem to be anything to bring them out this early. Unless they were getting ready to ride on a job perhaps . . .

Two men were at the fire in front of the cave, blowing on the embers to bring it back to life. One man went to gather kindling while the other coaxed a feather of smoke into a small flame, dropped a handful of dry grass on, and when it flared, added some twigs. By the time the other came back with bigger sticks he had a small fire going.

Langtry adjusted his peep-sight behind the breech, flipping it upright, adjusting the slide on the scale to the range he estimated to be about 50 yards.

The thundering boom of the big gun made Janet jump even though she was expecting it. She snapped her head around quickly to the men outside the

185

cave, saw them look up sharply — and then the one who had brought the kindling was suddenly somersaulting backwards, slammed several yards up the slope towards the cave mouth by the smashing impact of the huge bullet.

The shell case leapt out of the smoking breech as Langtry dropped the action open, slid home another cartridge, snapped it closed, and drew bead on the second outlaw. He started to his feet, but was only half-risen when he tumbled violently end over end, skidding right through the fire, scattering burning sticks and the coffee pot and skillet.

By then men were appearing in the cave mouth and at the door of the shack.

Langtry's Sharps boomed a third time and a man at the shack door was blown back inside out of sight. The other man froze, just long enough for the sniper to reload, and ducked back quickly. The rifle crashed and the girl saw a handful of splinters erupt from the plank wall beside the door; a dark, ragged blotch, which she realized must be a whole section of timber punched out, suddenly appeared. She knew the man inside would've been behind that section of wall when Langtry fired . . .

She ducked suddenly as guns hammered from the cave mouth and bullets ricocheted from the ridge. Janet brought her Henry around and fired off five fast shots towards the cave but the hammering fire continued to rake the ridge.

Langtry held his position and she thought he must have nerves of steel as he sighted coolly through his peepsight. She watched his finger curl round the double-set trigger, saw it jump very slightly as the first tension let off, and then his whole body jerked and twisted as the recoil rippled through him and she spun to look at the cave.

Rock chips erupted from the cave mouth as if smashed by a fourteen-pound sledge and a man's body briefly appeared, airborne, as it was hurled back into the darkness.

Someone shouted in alarm and she frowned puzzledly. But Langtry winked at her as he thumbed home another load, settled down and fired once more.

This time he shot above the ridge of rock, aiming into the dome of the cave. Even from here she heard the savage, snoring buzz of the huge bullet ricocheting around the cave.

A man screamed. By that time Langtry was shooting again. More snarling wasp-sounds, more screams — terror-stricken. She thought she heard a wild sob. Then someone started praying loudly, the words chopped off, running together, almost unintelligible. Hoarse. Panic-stricken. Screamed in utter fear, at the edge of death . . .

She was pale as she turned to Langtry. 'God, that's enough to make them give up, isn't it?'

'Best make sure,' he said casually, fired again, and once more she flinched at the sounds of terror and agony coming from inside the cave.

'The shack!' she cried suddenly, pointing, and he looked in that direction swiftly.

A man, doubled over, was making a run for the crude corral where the horses were milling and whinnying, frightened by the powerful sounds of the big gun. Langtry sighted, led him slightly, and the man's broken body skidded ten feet under the bottom corral rail.

He swung the smoking gun barrel back towards the shack, saw the splintered door closing, hit it with a shot that tore it off its hinges.

Then he gave his attention back to the cave, fired another shot into it and someone yelled, "*Nough*! For Chrissakes, man — '*nough*! We give up!'

'Throw out your guns!' Langtry called, and after a pause, two rifles and a pistol sailed over the bullet-shattered ridge and landed on the slope near the still body of the outlaw he had first shot.

'Watch the shack,' Langtry said to the

girl quietly, covered the cave mouth as he called, 'How many of you are there?'

'Just three . . . you kilt the rest, damn you!'

'Shooting better'n I thought. All right. I better see just three of you coming out — but I better see it right now.'

'He might be lying!' the girl hissed, without taking her eyes off the shack.

'Sure he is . . . ' He had removed his hat while he was shooting. Now he set it on the end of the barrel of the saddle carbine the girl had loaned him, lifted it slightly above the protecting ridge, and moved it towards the right. Through a gap in the rocks he saw three dishevelled men with their hands raised, coming out mighty slowly and very, very leery. He didn't do more than give them a brief glance.

Then he shifted his gaze behind them, to the dark cave mouth. A movement. Could have been a pack rat scurrying for cover. But it wasn't — it was a man's head as he rose to his knees behind the protecting ridge, throwing a rifle to his shoulder. He fired and Langtry's hat spun wildly off the carbine's barrel. He groaned loudly and the girl swung towards him in surprise and alarm.

When she saw he was all right, drawing a bead on the cave, she tightened her lips and waited for the roar of the big Sharps. She had only a few seconds to wait: the three men were grinning now, turning back towards the cave as a man stood up in there, smoking rifle in hand.

'You got him Chucky!' a man said, and then the Sharps' roar drowned him out and the man in the cave was blasted back out of sight.

Maybe out of existence . . .

The three men outside scattered, yelling in panic. Langtry let them go, reloaded quickly.

'You in there, Largo?' he called. 'If you are come on out — and die like a man!'

11

Mad Dog

They watched the cave closely from behind the protection of rocks, but nothing moved, no sounds at all came from it. The men sprawled around the hillside were motionless and bloody.

'Keep an eye on the shack,' Langtry told the girl, as he laid aside the heavy buffalo gun and took up the carbine, checking that the tubular magazine was full. He levered a shell into the breech. 'I managed to shoot the door off its hinges, but I think there was someone inside pulling it closed.'

'Then your bullet probably got him when it went through the door.'

'Just keep an eye on it.'

'Where are you going?'

'To check out the cave. That *hombre* on the slope yelled 'You got him

Chucky!' . . . I want to see if he meant Chuckaluck Magraw.'

The three men he had allowed to escape down the slope had circled back to the corrals, grabbed horses and high-tailed it to the narrow pass that led out of the valley.

She watched as he jammed his bullet-pierced hat on to his head and then checked his sixgun.

'You're a hard man to figure out, Buck Langtry . . . you shoot down half-a-dozen men in cold blood . . . '

'They deserved to die.'

'Yes, but you let three others ride out.'

'I didn't do them any favours. They're so scared they won't stop this side of the border. And they'll never sleep easy again, wondering when I'll be coming for them.'

'You *are* a cold-blooded son of a bitch, aren't you!'

'Blame it on life. It's made us all what we are.'

'Don't go deep on me!' She frowned,

puzzled. 'I'm not even sure why I-I'm showing concern over this.'

'You should've gone back when I suggested it.'

'No, you needed someone to watch your back.'

It mollified him some. 'Well, keep an eye on the shack now. Anyone comes out, shoot 'em.'

Then he was gone, rolling over the protective rim of rock and the next time she saw him he was approaching the cave from one side.

Watching Langtry, she missed seeing the man who climbed out of a rear window of the shack and then ran, crouched double, towards some boulders that were half-hidden behind a growth of brush . . .

She saw Langtry go into the cave fast, rolling in over the entrance, and was just turning back to the shack when she heard the racket of gunfire erupting from the cave.

Langtry was in mid-air when he saw something off to his left and he twisted violently, lifting the carbine and shooting towards the movement, even as a gunflash stabbed at him.

A bullet ricocheted around the domed roof of the cave and for a few moments he knew something of the terror that had gripped the outlaws when his big buffalo-killing bullets had bounced randomly off these same walls.

The gun fired at him again and this time the slug *thupped* into the short sandy slope. By then he had landed and he grunted with the jolt, sprawled on his stomach, already levering a fresh shell into the carbine's breech. He fired as the gun in the shadows stabbed at him a third time, didn't hear where the bullet went, but knew his own had found its target.

There was no mistaking the sound of the lead smacking into human flesh. The sound was followed by an explosive grunt of pain and then a body tumbled into sight, sprawling face down.

Langtry approached warily, cocked

carbine out ahead and slanted down, covering the man every inch of the way. He saw the blood soaking the back of the man's shirt, the way his right arm hung twisted and useless, and he figured this was the man who had stayed behind when the other three had come out with their hands up.

He got a boot toe under the man's good shoulder and heaved him on to his back. It was Chuckaluck Magraw and he was, amazingly, still alive. Not by much, but there was a small spark there, enough for the man to try to curse Langtry.

The rancher saw that the Sharps' bullet had shattered Magraw's right shoulder. It said something for the man's courage, or hate, that he had stayed alive — and quiet — enough until Langtry entered the cave before making his last try.

'No wonder you missed, Chucky,' Langtry said. 'You never were much of a shot with your left hand.' He squatted by the dying man, seeing the frothy blood-bubbles on the man's lips. 'You're all through, Magraw . . . even if there was a sawbones here he couldn't do anything for you.'

Chuckaluck glared, fighting for breath.

'Where's Largo? Come on, what good's it gonna do you keeping it to yourself?'

Magraw's mouth moved, but only unintelligible sounds came out.

'One more time, then I'm going, Chucky, you'll have to die alone.'

Alarm flared in the outlaw's pain-filled eyes and Langtry knew he had guessed right: Magraw didn't want to die alone. He wanted human company up till the last breath, even if it was that of a man he hated. Langtry had seen it happen a hundred times during the war: hard, bitter men who kept to themselves, cared nothing for human company. Yet without exception they had all pleaded for someone to stay with them when they were dying.

Magraw's hand touched his arm

weakly and Langtry looked down, saw the plea in the man's eyes.

'Sure, I'll stay, Chucky, but I'd sure admire to know where I can find Ed Largo.'

He had to lean down until his ear almost touched those blood-flecked lips to hear what the man said.

'Shack . . . '

Langtry stiffened. Neither of the two men he had shot at the shack had been Largo . . . he must have been the man still inside when he'd blasted the door off its hinges.

He looked down at Magraw, surprised to see that the man was dead: he hadn't heard the death rattle or any other sound. The man had simply passed over.

He stood stiffly, saw one more dead man on one side of the cave and then walked to the entrance, glancing towards the shack.

'Janet, Chuckaluck says Largo's the one in the shack.'

'She knows, Langtry!'

Two figures rose on the slope, two figures blended almost into one . . . Janet Jarvis, her slim body being used as a shield by Ed Largo who had a cocked sixgun pressed against her head.

Largo leaned over her shoulder and ran his tongue up the side of her face. He chuckled as she wrenched away.

'You know 'zactly where I am, don't you, sweetie?'

Langtry said nothing: Largo wasn't the kind who would heed a plea of any kind. He would relish it as a demonstration of the victim's rising fear.

'Hey, Langtry, lot of folk've underestimated you, I bet. You're good, man, *damn* good! Wish I didn't hate your guts so much. We'd make a great team, you an' me.'

'Sorry, Largo. Not interested.'

Largo laughed, tightening his grip on the writhing girl. 'Nah, me neither . . . I'm just talkin' while I figure out what to do with you this time. I liked that anthill idea, never figured you'd survive, but kinda glad you did. I don't

199

mind having another crack at you
. . . an' this time I got sweetie here to
help me out, huh?'

'Why don't you put her aside and
then you and me can have at it?'

Largo grinned. 'That 'die like a man'
hogwash you was yelling about before?'
He swiftly shook his head. 'I got no
plans for dyin' at all for a long time yet,
Langtry. An' why would I be loco
enough to throw this away when I ain't
even sampled it?'

Janet stiffened and Langtry was
surprised to see her eyes narrow: he
might have expected them to widen in
rising terror as she realized the import
of Largo's words, but no — her face
hardened and he looked away quickly
in case his own expression tipped Largo
that something might be wrong.

'So that's how it's going to be?' he
said flatly.

Largo bared his teeth. 'Always the
genn'lman, Langtry. Women an' kids
first with me!' He laughed and
Langtry didn't like the sound of it.

The man really *was* loco.

As he watched, Largo twisted his fingers in Janet's hair and she gave a small cry as he yanked her head back. He kissed her slim throat and that was the biggest mistake he ever made.

The girl seemed to literally explode all over Largo.

She wrenched her head down, losing a little hair in the process, and sank her teeth into Largo's stubbled cheek. Blood flowed and he growled as he wrenched away. Janet spat in his face and he shook his head, as she rammed against him, knee rising, knocking him sprawling.

But he was an old hand at rough-and-tumble and even as he fell, he swept her legs out from under her and she sat down with a thump. Largo tried to twist towards her, saw Langtry closing in and spun back, sixgun blasting.

Langtry dropped flat and fired the carbine, threw the short-barrelled rifle at the man as he spun away, dragging out his Colt. The girl knew enough to get well clear and Largo snapped a shot at her as she rolled away. Then wrenched back towards Langtry.

The rancher came up on hands and knees and hurled himself at the killer, not wanting bullets flying around with the girl still so close. He struck with his gun barrel, felt it jar against Largo's wrist and the man's gun dropped. But instantly he threw dirt into Langtry's face and the rancher ducked instinctively, hearing the gravel rattle against the stiff felt of his hat. When he looked up, Largo's boot was swinging straight for the middle of his face. He had lost his gun. He flung himself aside and the boot tore his ear. He grabbed the man's leg, heaved, bringing Largo down again. The outlaw struck backwards and his spur rowel laid a line of blood across Langtry's face. He spun away, scrabbled to his feet on the slope and thrust up to meet Largo as the man charged, a rock in one hand.

His face was almost black with fury,

his eyes starting out of his head, spittle flying. Langtry had seen mad dogs look less frightening. He ducked under the rock as it swung at his head, grabbed the outlaw by the crotch and the neck and roared as he lifted him above his head. His arms quivered and he stumbled a little as Largo writhed and kicked, trying to upset his stance.

Langtry spun and flung the man from him into the rocks. Largo yelled as he thudded down amongst them, banging his head, jamming one arm and shoulder, wrenching his back and a knee. He moaned sickly and looked up through a mask of blood, saw Langtry clambering over the rocks to get at him.

For the first time in his adult life, Largo knew raw fear.

He saw the murderous look on the rancher's face and knew that he had underestimated the man more than anyone . . . he should never have threatened the girl, he knew that now. But it was too late.

Half-crippled, he threw himself over

the rocks and fell sprawling, crawling out of them on the far side as Langtry came charging up. He rolled down the slope, gasping in pain as his injuries touched the ground. But all he cared about was getting away. The shack! There was a sawn-off shotgun in there that Bart had tried to bring into play. If he could get to it, he would take care of Langtry — a lot faster than he meant to, but a man could die painfully from a well-placed shotgun blast — and then he would return to the girl . . .

He couldn't straighten and the hot pain seared his bruised spine and torn muscles. He limped badly and Langtry wasn't even hurrying now as he leapt from one rock to the other. The son of a bitch *knew* he would catch up.

The thought spurred him on and he sobbed, holding his injured shoulder, feeling bones grating. Blood dripped into his eyes, blurring his vision. One leg buckled and he put out a hand quickly to keep from going all the way down. He staggered drunkenly and felt the sickness of fear welling up in him as Langtry came striding relentlessly after him, face set in those deadly lines, looking unstoppable.

Largo somehow found the power to increase his staggering pace, saw that the shack was only a few yards away now. He sobbed again, gasping, head spinning, one hand actually reaching out. The splintered door lay half over the stoop and it clattered as he lurched on to it and began to laugh as he sensed victory.

Then he stopped dead, leaning forward, balanced precariously on the damaged door.

His sudden scream was drowned by the double-barrelled blast of a shotgun.

Largo's body was lifted clear and flung through the bullet-splintered doorway, skidding a yard or two before coming to a halt.

Langtry stopped in his tracks, looking in bewilderment at Largo's buckshot-torn body.

12

Die — Any Way

Langtry heard the girl call him and he turned slightly away from Largo's body, but kept an eye on the door of the shack as he crouched low behind a pile of branches awaiting breaking-up into kindling.

'Throw me the carbine or my sixgun. Pronto!'

She was in control quickly and looked around on the ground, found his carbine and snatched it up, also a sixgun lying in a patch of sand. She came around the pile of rocks and ran, crouching, towards him. He swore: he had meant for her to stay behind the rocks and just to throw him the guns. But she dropped beside him and he took the carbine, levered in a shell as she asked, 'What happened?'

'Someone blasted Largo as he went into the shack — whether by mistake or otherwise I dunno.'

She grimaced and looked away from Largo's torn body, holding the Colt pistol. 'I'll cover you.'

He nodded at her curtly, then started towards the shack, moving sideways so that he was not in line with the doorway, coming up on one wall. There was a glassless window above him, the shutter down, though it was splintered by bullets. Warily, he lifted his head and squinted through a bullet hole. He couldn't see anything at first and then caught a movement and made out a man's leg. It twitched. He tightened his grip on the carbine as he moved around a little so as to get a better view. He tensed as he saw the smoking, sawn-off shotgun lying beside a man who was sitting up against the opposite wall. One hand lay limply on the weapon, the other was pressed into his midriff above the belt buckle and it was very bloody.

Langtry didn't recognize him, but he

could see the man was pretty well past being a danger to anyone.

Just the same he approached the door cautiously, then went in quickly, carbine braced against his hip.

'Don't try anything!'

The wounded man looked at him with lidded eyes. A dark line of semi-dried blood ran from the corner of his mouth to the line of his narrow jaw.

'Did . . . I . . . get . . . him?' he rasped, and the words stopped Langtry in his tracks.

'Blew him to Kingdom Come.'

The man almost smiled although it was obvious he was in real pain. Then a shadow darkened the doorway and Langtry jumped aside, spinning. The girl gasped at his speed and the sudden threat of that carbine. He relaxed, swallowing a curse.

'Thought I told you to stay put.'

She looked past him at the wounded man. 'That's Bart Venters — Largo's second-in-command.'

Venters curled a lip. 'Once. Somethin' happened to him in that . . . Laredo jail. When he come out he was . . . even more loco than before. Treated me like dirt. Chuckaluck, too. Took over the gang. Killed a couple when they . . . argued. He shot — me.'

Langtry arched his eyebrows. 'What for?'

'I wanted to get out . . . when you started . . . pickin' everyone off. Ed said 'no'. Sent out Lucky and Jude but you nailed them. I figured to go out the rear window but he . . . put a bullet in my back. When I fell he put another in my . . . gut. I tried to get the sawn-off but . . . ' Suddenly his lips twitched. 'Well, I did get it . . . eventually, eh?'

The girl knelt beside the man but didn't have enough strength to pull his hand away from the belly wound. He moaned.

'Leave it!' His breathing was a series of gasps now. 'Everything'll come out if I move it . . . '

'I might be able to help.'

He moved his head wearily from side to side. 'Too late. Just glad I . . . busted Largo . . .'

'How did you know I was back at my ranch?' Langtry asked suddenly. 'You have a man watching?'

Venters looked at him blankly and Langtry asked again, impatiently.

'Before you blew the dam . . . you must've had someone watching. Which means you knew I'd gotten off the anthill. It just doesn't seem to make sense and hasn't been sitting easy in my mind all along.' He saw the girl looking at him strangely. 'Well, why would they set someone to watch my place when they figured I was already dying on the anthill? Sounds to me like someone from Laredo or the valley sent Largo word.'

'Maybe they checked after they ambushed the posse.'

'No,' gasped Venters before Langtry could reply. 'An' we never sent no one to watch for you. Largo said if you survived, the posse'd've sent you into

Laredo. But no one wanted to get that close to the law to find out. So, we figured just to wait and see what happened.'

'And blew my dam just for the hell of it.'

Venters' face was contorted with pain, but suddenly it ironed-out and there was a flash of life in his eyes as he looked up at Langtry.

'You're . . . crazy! No one blew your . . . dam! Largo wanted *you* if you was still alive. He was a kinda backasswards *hombre*. Got some sorta kick outa makin' hisself wait to find out for sure. But . . . we never blew no dam. We were layin' low . . . after that ambush Largo made us pull. Scared they'd send in the army.'

'He's telling the truth, Buck.'

The rancher nodded. There was no point in Venters lying now. The man had only a short time left in this life.

'It had to be someone not connected with Largo,' she added.

'Yeah — ' he said slowly, battered,

211

scarred face hardening. 'Someone else who . . . figured Largo or Chuckaluck Magraw would be blamed for it . . . '

★　★　★

Venters died without speaking again.

It was an unpleasant job wrapping Largo's body in a tarp, and Chuckaluck wasn't much better, but Langtry got the chore done and tied them across two horses from the corrals. Then he carried or dragged the dead men into the shack and poured coal oil over them and the shack itself and set it on fire. It was the best he could do under the circumstances. He and the pale-faced girl rode out of the hidden valley, leading the horses carrying the dead men before the stench became too great.

It was a silent ride back to Laredo and a couple of times he caught the girl looking at him a bit strangely. She had stitched the spur-rowel cut on his face with ordinary sewing thread she had in a small repair kit she carried in her saddle-bags, but he could feel that it wasn't really holding and figured he would end up with a fairly large scar.

Not that it bothered him: his face reflected the kind of life he'd led, and one more scar wouldn't make that much difference, even if it would be more prominent than his others.

'You want to go back to your spread, I can handle the chore of taking these two in to Red Satterlee,' he suggested, when they came to the escarpment at the edge of the Topaz Breaks.

'No, I'll come in.'

He smiled crookedly. 'Don't trust me, huh?'

She snapped her head around. 'I trust you, Buck Langtry, but I'm still trying to figure you out. You're quite a complex man, you know.'

'Always figured I was a pretty simple kinda feller. Some things you did, others you didn't — no matter what. And that's about it.'

She almost smiled. 'There're worse ways to be. I thought I'd misjudged you when you shot all those men down. I thought you were a coldblooded killer underneath. Now, I see your side. Those men not only died for you, they died *because* of you, and you had to balance up the books as it were. Am I right?'

'Don't forget the reward.'

She tightened her lips. 'I wish you wouldn't do that!'

He looked at her blankly. 'What?'

'Belittle your motives . . . ' Then suddenly she smiled. 'But I suppose that's part of your charm.'

Surprise crossed his face. 'Charm? Me? Lady, you must be thinking of ten other fellers. *Charm* is the one thing I've never had . . . '

Her glance was sidelong. 'That's all you know,' she said, so quietly that he asked her to repeat it but she shook her head and said it was nothing.

Then they skirted her ranch and took the lonely trail into Laredo.

Their arrival caused something of a stir and quite a crowd gathered and followed them down the street to the law office.

Red Satterlee, leaning on his cane still, was already in the doorway, some townsman having run on ahead to tell him about the small procession. He stomped across the walk as Langtry and the girl dismounted.

'Is that who I hope it is under the tarps?' Red asked, and Langtry went to the horses carrying the dead men and flipped back the canvas corners.

The crowd pressed closer, some gasping as they recognized Chuckaluck Magraw and Ed Largo. Red Saterlee scratched at his stringy sandy hair.

'Well, I'll be dogged if you ain't gone and done it, Buck, but the little lady here looks as if she's been through hell and high water, too. Something happen out at her ranch I ought to know about?'

'I'm here, Sheriff,' Janet said curtly. 'Don't talk about me as if I were across the street!'

'Sorry, ma'am. Question still stands.'

'Only thing that happened was that Miz Jarvis volunteered to lead me into outlaw country, Red, so we split any re-ward right down the middle.'

That got the crowd murmuring and staring and nudging each other, but Janet had no trouble ignoring them or meeting their stares squarely. *She's got a lotta grit*, thought Langtry.

'We best get these fellers to the undertaker's, Red,' he said, and the man in question pushed through the crowd, bringing two helpers with him carrying old doors.

In minutes, the dead men were carried away and the sheriff dispersed the crowd and gestured to Langtry and the girl to come into his office.

'This is where the paperwork starts,' the sheriff said, sitting awkwardly and with a grunt.

'You get it going, Red, I've got some business to attend to.'

Satterlee snapped his head up as he took some papers from a desk drawer, saw the girl was looking tautly at Langtry, too.

'What kinda business?' he asked suspiciously.

'Need to find a couple of things out . . . I'll be back.'

'Buck . . . ' He turned in the doorway as the girl spoke his name. 'Don't be long. Sooner we get these claims away the sooner we can collect our money.'

He smiled slowly. 'Knew you'd be concerned about that.'

She smiled in return. 'That and other things. We need your signature, too, you know.' Meaning, *come back safe*.

He laughed shortly and Red Satterlee frowned, looking in bewilderment from one to the other. Then, as Langtry made to step out to the street, the sheriff said quietly, 'Before you go, Buck, the bank sent a man out to your place to have you sign some papers about a new agreement you'd made with Whit Capstick. Man came back and said your place was flooded, turned into mud that was hardenin' and would break a hoss's leg tryin' to get to your front door.'

Langtry nodded slowly. 'Dam burst. Just what I needed on top of everything else.'

'Buck, that bank feller skirted around all that mud, got himself up on to that hogback just south of your cabin. He said the dam was gone all right, but he could see blast-marks on some of the rocks at the side.'

'Blast marks?'

'Quit that, Buck! It don't work with me. Did you blow up that dam for some reason I ain't been able to figure?'

'No, I didn't blow it up, Red. Matter of fact, that's why I went after Ed Largo so soon.' He was deliberately vague.

'*He* blew it?'

'Made sense to think so. He waited till I got back, more or less recovered from the anthill, when I'd be thinking things might start to get back to normal, and then he blew the dam to ruin me.'

'He was a mean sonuver, all right! You get him to admit to it?'

'No. Bart Venters gunned him down before I had a chance to ask him about it . . . '

Langtry swivelled his eyes to the girl and whatever was in his gaze she read silently and gave the bare suggestion of a nod.

The sheriff was bewildered. 'Venters nailed Largo . . . ? But I thought Venters was his next-in-charge?'

'Janet can tell you all about it. I'll make a full statement when I get back, Red.'

'Now wait up! This isn't as clear-cut as I figured when you first rode in.'

But Langtry was gone and Satterlee smothered a curse. Janet smiled at him.

'I can give you the details, Sheriff.'

★   ★   ★

Doc Ferris opened the door to Langtry's knock and the rancher immediately saw that the man wasn't his usual cool calm and collected self.

219

The medico's face was drawn, tight-lipped, and his nostrils flared. His eyes were restless, not quite meeting Langtry's gaze.

'You all right, Doc?'

'Yes, yes, Buck. What is it? I'm very busy . . . Pink Hardiman's busted a leg and it's a greenstick break. I'm in the middle of trying to set it.'

Langtry half-turned towards the gate. 'Noticed his horse hitched to your fence. Figured he must've been visiting Mitch Tyrell — who's the man I want to see.'

He started forward, but the doctor blocked him. 'You're too late, I'm afraid, Buck. Mitch is gone.'

'Gone where?' Langtry was puzzled. 'I figured he was gonna be laid-up for quite some time.'

Doc gave him a stiff, false grin. 'Never can tell with some of you range men. Mitch is mighty tough and he's made a good recovery. Went back to the Double T yesterday — Swede Andersen picked him up in a buckboard.'

The sawbones was talking too much. Normally, Will Ferris was concise, almost abrupt when giving information about anything, especially his patients' health.

'Buckboard, eh? Then he couldn't've been too spry if he wasn't able to fork a horse.'

'Uh — no, not quite well enough for that, though he likely will be in a day or two. Now, I'm sorry, Buck, but if you want to see Mitch Tyrell, you'd best ride out to Double T.'

'Yeah, guess I'd better . . . Thanks, Doc.'

As Ferris closed the door he leaned his head close to Langtry and whispered, 'Don't go by way of Rattler Creek.'

The door closed and Langtry was left staring at the peeling paint just a few inches in front of his nose.

Don't go by way of Rattler Creek. What the hell? That was the regular trail from town to Double T.

He began walking slowly back up the

path. The creek was a wide, shallow stream overhung with willows, banks dotted with clumps of cat-tails. The crossing that led to the trail out to Tyrell's Double T spread was down in a dip between high, eroded clay walls. It was a favourite picnic spot for townsfolk at weekends — but it would also make a fine spot for an ambush . . .

Damn! If Doc was warning him that Swede Andersen was lying in wait for him, why did he have to whisper in that way? *Oh-oh*! Pink Hardiman! The man was one of Tyrell's hardcases, was always in brawls, liked beating-up on people weaker than himself, men *or* women.

Langtry knew the man had gone on the trail drive but there had been plenty of time for him to return. Come to think of it, although Pink was mighty tough — even if he did favour pink-coloured shirts and underwear — Langtry didn't figure he was tough enough to ride in all the way from the valley with a greenstick break in his leg . . . few men could manage such a thing.

Which meant that Doc Ferris had been lying, something Langtry couldn't come to terms with.

Doc was a mighty honest man, wouldn't lie if someone held a gun to his head. Well, maybe then . . .

'Judas! That's just about what must've happened!'

He spoke half-aloud and a couple of ladies passing by on the walk as he turned on to the main drag gave him a wide berth, thinking he was just another drunk.

He turned quickly down the alley between the barber's shop and the druggist's, hurried through the slop and piles of rubbish to the vacant lot at the rear where the wheelwright parked the wagons and stacked the wheels he was waiting to work on.

They gave him cover as he crawled beneath them and lay in the long grass where he could see the doctor's house. He had to change position so he could see the infirmary window but the curtains were drawn. He was about to move again when a man passed by another window — a man wearing a pink shirt — walking briskly and without a sign of a limp.

That was enough for him. He rolled out from beneath the sheltering wagon, ran across the vacant lot at an angle that would bring him out at the rear of the doctor's house. Breathing a little hard and feeling a trickle of blood ooze from under the cotton pad on his spur-torn face, he slipped into the doctor's yard, palming up his sixgun.

In minutes, he stood in the coolness of the kitchen where something savoury bubbled in a pot on the big wood range. Then he spun sharply towards a sound at the passage door, gun coming up, hammer starting to cock. But he froze the movement when he saw it was Ferris himself. The doctor's eyes widened and his face darkened with anger as he stepped quickly into the kitchen, hissing, 'Get out! I didn't expect you to come back *here*!'

'Where's Pink, Doc? He still behind you with a gun like when you were at the front door?'

'Buck, you have to go! They'll kill you!' Ferris was pale and trembling now, looked around nervously. 'They have my wife locked in the root cellar. If I don't do as they say, Pink'll go down there and . . . '

Langtry laid a hand on the worried medico's arm. 'Just tell me where he is, Doc. I'll take care of Pink Hardiman.'

'He . . . he's in the infirmary with Mitch. I'm supposed to be getting them whiskey.'

'Do it, Doc.'

Langtry covered the door as Ferris hurried to a cupboard, knelt and brought out a bottle of whiskey.

'Hurry it up, goddamnit!' Mitch Tyrell called impatiently and Langtry ushered the doctor out into the passage, followed, crouching.

'Look out!' Ferris cried suddenly. 'The stairs!'

He dropped flat, hurling the whiskey bottle as he did so. Langtry glimpsed Pink Hardiman halfway up the stairs and them the hardcase's gun hammered and lead ploughed into the floor between the rancher's boots. He threw himself to one side, firing, hitting on his back, skidding across the polished wood.

The slide saved him from the two shots that Hardiman triggered swiftly between the stair rails, shouting, 'It's Langtry, boss!'

He suddenly placed one hand on the rail and jumped down into the room. Langtry brought up from his slide against the wall, got his gun up and slapped at the hammer spur with the edge of his left hand. Hardiman's blocky body shuddered and he landed heavily. But he started up, his face dull, pink shirt front blotched with bright red. He stumbled forward, firing wild, barely able to hold his sixgun, dead on his feet.

Langtry put his last bullet into him

and the man went down and stayed down this time.

The rancher hurriedly reloaded, seeing the white-faced doctor getting to his feet. 'Go to your wife, Doc. Set her free and get out of here.'

The doctor ran back into the kitchen to fumble at the root-cellar door. Langtry, gun reloaded now, ran for a padded blanket box sitting at an angle to the parlour wall on an Indian floormat. It was constructed of heavy cedar planks and had been decorated with folk art. He got behind it, manoeuvred it on to the polished floor and ran with it ahead of him towards the infirmary door.

He released it and it smashed open the door like a runaway wagon and a shotgun roared from inside, buckshot raking across the cedar planks, splintering them.

Langtry dived headlong through the doorway and glimpsed the bandaged Tyrell standing beside the bed, cocking the hammer of the smoking

Greener's second barrel.

The rancher landed atop the blanket box and its shattered timbers collapsed under him, spilling him to the floor at the same time saving him from the shotgun's charge of buckshot.

He rolled off, kicking at the splintered timbers, saw Tyrell snatching a Sheriff's Special from under the pillow ... Langtry lifted his upper body, shooting fast at an upward angle, three evenly-spaced shots.

Tyrell lifted to his toes, spun, his gun exploding into the pillow and filling the room with feathers as he fell across the bed, staining Mrs Ferris's white sheets red ...

He slid slowly to the floor with a heavy, lifeless thud.

★ ★ ★

The sheriff came with Janet and as many of the townsfolk who could crush into the doctor's house before Red Satterlee roared 'Goddamnit!

That's enough!'

Ferris backed Langtry's story and said he had been present when Tyrell had sent out Swede Andersen to set up an ambush at Rattler Creek. The injured, worried Tyrell had added, 'We've got to kill Langtry before he kills us — and he *will*! It's obvious he's found out we blew his dam . . . '

Red Satterlee grabbed three hard-muscled townsmen who worked in the lumber yard, hastily deputized them and told them to get out to Rattler Creek crossing and bring in Swede Anderson. 'If he resists, shoot him — but I expect to see him; dead or alive, by sundown! Now, git!'

Satterlee wiped his face with his neckerchief while leaning on his cane. 'Well, with that settled, looks like this job might be tolerably peaceful after all . . . '

However, they didn't find Swede waiting in ambush for Langtry. The man had stopped at his own ranch, grabbed some money, and made a run for it in a buckboard. There was a heavy rainstorm that night. He crashed, was impaled on a lightning-struck tree, and lived just long enough to admit he had helped blow up Langtry's dam on Tyrell's orders.

* * *

Downstairs, after the crowd had dispersed and they were walking back towards the main part of town, Langtry said to Janet at his side, 'You gonna move out, or spruce up your ranch ready for when your husband comes home?'

She stopped abruptly and he had walked on a couple of steps before he realized it. He turned to face her, saw her white teeth tugging at her bottom lip.

'There's something I have to tell you, Buck — ' He waited in silence and she took a deep breath, adding, 'My husband is dead. He died in jail two years ago.'

His stare was thoughtful more than surprised. 'Uh-*huh*,' was all he said.

'I just allowed everyone to think he was still alive. It seemed like some form of protection in a way, having someone in the background who would eventually come home . . . '

'I can savvy that,' he said, and she knew he was sincere.

'I'm sorry I lied to you, but, well, now I think you have a right to know.'

'Dunno about a right but I 'preciate you telling me. Anyway, *what* are you going to do about your ranch?'

'I'm not going back there.'

'You'll be leaving the valley then?'

She felt a strange surge as she heard the concern — anxiety — in his voice. She hesitated.

'I — didn't say that.'

'Well . . . ' The word dragged on into silence and it seemed that neither knew how to break it, but then he said, 'Well, I've got plenty of land if you want to settle around Melody Creek . . . '

'You're offering to sell me land?'

He shrugged. 'Buy if you want to, or share . . . ?'

She started a little. 'Share . . . ?'

He said nothing as their gazes locked.

Just waited for her reply, a kind of expectant, crooked smile on his battered face, one eyebrow arched quizzically.

THE END

We do hope that you have enjoyed reading this large print book.

Did you know that all of our titles are available for purchase?

We publish a wide range of high quality large print books including:
Romances, Mysteries, Classics, General Fiction, Non Fiction and Westerns.

Special interest titles available in large print are:
The Little Oxford Dictionary Music Book, Song Book Hymn Book, Service Book

Also available from us courtesy of Oxford University Press:
Young Readers' Dictionary (large print edition) Young Readers' Thesaurus (large print edition)

For further information or a free brochure, please contact us at:
Ulverscroft Large Print Books Ltd., The Green, Bradgate Road, Anstey, Leicester, LE7 7FU, England. Tel: (00 44) **0116 236 4325 Fax:** (00 44) **0116 234 0205**

Soon the ... men would be on its long ... down the Missouri River ... all Saul Rhymer had ... ay the ... broke ... g. He ... the mountain ... of gold ... bill and again at ... he cards in his hand. Then looking around the table, he produced the deed ... goldmine in Montana. 'Let's play poker!' But little did he know how that journey back to St Louis would change his life so drastically.